POOL MAN

A NIGHTMARE IN RIVERTON NOVEL

DAN MCDOWELL

Black Rose Writing | Texas

ISBN: 978-1-68433-999-0
PUBLISHED BY BLACK ROSE WRITING
www.blackrosewriting.com

Printed in the United States of America
Suggested Retail Price (SRP) $18.95

Pool Man is printed in EB Garamond

*As a planet-friendly publisher, Black Rose Writing does its best to eliminate unnecessary waste to reduce paper usage and energy costs, while never compromising the reading experience. As a result, the final word count vs. page count may not meet common expectations.

This one is for Nate. A man who could never go a day in his life without a smile, a joke, or the last laugh. I love you, brother.

SPECIAL THANKS

Much appreciation to my lovely wife, Tiffiny— for her continued feedback and transparent support amid hare-brained ideas— always brave enough to challenge and bold enough to support quirky exploits into dark and unknown places.

At the genesis of this work, I'd like to thank my mother for her detailed eyes and valued critique. To my father for helping me ponder depth and emotion to characters. And to my brother, Nate, for his creative inputs. Furthermore, I'd like to thank my alpha and beta readers.

At this work's exodus (and there certainly was one of those), a shout out to my editor, Michelle, who helped me bring it across the finish line at feverish speeds and helped make this project become 3D.

Thanks to all of you that have left feedback on *Level Zero* and *Oak Hollow*. From one star to five, they all matter!

Thanks to my family and friends for their support, and to the Black Rose Writing family of authors. And, finally, thanks to Reagan Rothe and the team at Black Rose Writing for encouraging more nightmares in Riverton.

POOL MAN

"Fragments are an artform, commas, your friend, and run on sentences
make your grammar teachers and mothers go nuts."

"Why, you do not even know what will happen tomorrow. What is your life?
You are a mist that appears for a little while and then vanishes."
–JAMES 4:14

CHAPTER ONE
FLOATER

1991

A body floats atop the water, its color eradicated, its character erased. I can't do anything about it, though. He's not the first man to be left for dead in a swimming pool, and certainly not the last.

No. I don't have some quandary running through my head about the right and wrong, no more than the average man, anyway. Only an unrefined peace of mind that good things happen to good people, sometimes. And bad things happen to good people, sometimes. What do I know? Perhaps the guy was no good at all, and his death's completely justified.

There's no indicator of his origin, how he ended up in the pool, or why he's dead, and maybe it's not my concern. He lays there motionless, only the water to buoy him around as he faces the sky and day breaks upon us. His freshly pressed jacket, ruined by chlorine, his button-down shirt and tie, soaked and soon sun bleached. Truth is, the unsightly corpse's indicators of success are all gone. An unsubtle reminder that pursuits for wealth in the deep end don't always end well. One can only wonder so much about this sort of situation. Of course, I want to know what happened. If life's but a vapor, we have two options: own every day like it's our last, or run in fear, knowing we'll one day meet our end, sometimes interesting, and sometimes not. And that's it.

I can hope an unspoken eulogy from a stranger gives the man closure, but I can't say for certain. He's still there, still dead.

I do a lot of this sort of musing to get by, making my lonely days and nights more bearable. I feel smarter, too, although I'm a few brain cells shorter than I was yesterday. It's that imperfect blend of the cynical, the rhetorical, the philosophical, and the comical, whiplashing each other in a barroom brawl— a hackneyed accountant and cruise ship comedian perfecting their offbeat tango across piles of broken glass.

That's as fluffy as my mental prose gets, I swear. I guess I'm admitting I ponder about like anybody else does to keep their sanity. I'm just trying to scrape by. So, when I'm not cracking jokes to bust stress, working to solve the world's problems, or pontificating to my one-armed audience of one, I'm cleaning pools. It's not a great living, but it's enough.

Yes, the man's still floating. He's just a hollow, soggy shell at this point. As the sky reflects on his lifeless eyes, I can say with absolute certainty, he didn't die by drowning, nor an accident. This is murder.

***

I move toward the business responsible, The Oak Hollow Hotel. I've got to report this... development to Jerry Greenwich. This may be our last visit—or, at least, the final one with me an employee. I don't know. I wouldn't call it my fault, but the pool's on my watch. I've handled it for years. In the 70s, it was the city pool—kept up well, and with plenty of patterned bikinis and swim trunks, summer eats and drinks gracing the poolside, and me keeping watch of the chemicals and the area's cleanliness. In the early 80s, it was a failing apartment complex pool where the yuppies, druggies, and cronies all united under the sun in its rolling waves. Not long after it went under, a peculiar entrepreneur took over the place, employing a bunch of degenerates to tell horror stories over the phone. It was odd, but caught on well. And he let them live here, too. Sometimes, these people would come down for a dip, their venereal diseases crossing streams, and me hoping and praying the chemicals I treated it with would be enough. Most of the time, not. Thankfully it was short-lived. The city took it back over again after that. A few weeks ago, a deal was inked, and the pool once again belongs to the hotel. I'm told this swimming hole's been around since the 40s, sometime after World War II. As for the property, it's had a bloody past, but that's another story for another day.

My heart's racing, my mind wandering in every direction but the one it needs to. I can't let anyone see the body. It wouldn't be fair. You can't unsee the dead. I consider my forthcoming fate, all but sealed. And it is indeed sealed. Despite the talks of checks and balances, processes and procedures, and all the many ways we can prevent this sort of thing from happening, human error is to blame sometimes. And, of course, the one night I forget to padlock the gate, this happens.

I walk through the lobby and down into the basement, tapping on Jerry's door.

His gruff voice sounds uncaffeinated and worn. "Yeah? Who is it?"

"Mr. Greenwich, it's Greg Preakle. I need to talk to you, sir."

"Preakle? Come on in."

I pop the door open, an immediate musty smell hitting me as Jerry puffs a cigar. His ugly face is tattered, probably too much smoking. I don't fancy spending time in here, certainly not with him. The aquamarine curtains in the office are dreadful— his disheveled desk, as low a priority as the dirt beneath his fingernails. And there's a lot of that.

I search for the right words.

"Sir, there's a... a problem with the pool."

He scowls at me, shaking his head as he adjusts a large stack of paperwork and checks his watch.

"And what's that? I've got things to get to."

I check over my shoulder and take a deep breath.

"Just come out and say it already," he interrupts.

I sigh. "There's a dead man out there."

"A what?"

"A man is dead in the pool, sir."

Greenwich's face turns pasty. The timbre of his voice becomes subdued. "That's what I thought you said. Well, let's deal with it, then, and try not to turn this into a big scene."

He motions me out of the room, staring at the nub hovering above what's left of my right arm, just above my would-be elbow. No prosthetic, just a fashion statement. I look at the door handle opposite me, reaching across awkwardly to push it open.

Greenwich picks up the phone and whispers, "I'm calling 911."

I move through the basement, an uninteresting space with dusty church pews, a large wood paneled television with feet, and a barber shop pole that no longer spins. There are a couple of apartments down here, too, but I'm not one of the lucky few to stay onsite. And lucky is a word I use cautiously. I suppose my role as Pool Man isn't essential enough to the operation to score a benefit like that, anyway.

As I've mentioned, I've watched this place wax and wane through the years, changing hands over and over, and arrived at the conclusion that spending too much time in the building seems more harmful than good. Weird things happen. People end up dead. And, inevitably, the place beckons more.

I work my way up the steps, slowed down by my disability but never set back. Naturally, the railing up the stairs is opposite my working arm. I'm used to it by now.

Greenwich catches up with me, making our ascent resemble a herd of elephants. "They're sending an ambulance and the cops," he says, huffing and puffing. "Did you recognize this guy?"

"I don't know, sir. It seems like the body was dumped. Never drowned, just left for dead."

Greenwich clicks his teeth as we go across the lobby, its ornate décor slowly coming back together after years of decline. "It's never that simple, Greg. Never."

"I know," I say, pulling the front door of the hotel open and moving toward the pool, "but you know how the police can be about Precinct Three. They always want everything as open and shut as possible."

He nods. "I have my hunches about that, but there's a time and place for those discussions. It's not here. And it's not with you…"

My stomach churns as we get closer, knowing the ugly stiff's still out there waiting for us. As we near the pool, Jerry's face sours. He pulls the gate open in a rush. "Just peachy!"

The look on his face tells me I'm screwed, and he is, too.

"I don't answer to the most likeable group of investors, Greg. We've got the ribbon cutting next week, and I'm here shit out of luck with a dead man to answer for."

A few minutes later, an ambulance arrives, and the paramedics hop out the back. I loiter around, hoping to stay out of it. From a distance, I assume Greenwich is giving a statement of our withering discovery.

I guess he's done. He walks toward me, dragging his feet. There's nothing new about that.

"Take the day off, Greg," he says. "I'll handle the rest. The less we make of this, the fewer questions we'll get. Good, bad, or ugly... this hotel's got to keep her best foot forward for opening day."

My dislike for Jerry drops a little. It's apparent he's said nothing to implicate me in the man's death— just what most of us would hope a boss would do in this unfortunate situation. Whether that's actually for my sake or to keep the hotel out of the news, who knows? As of this moment, I'm another day gainfully employed, and that's what matters. I don't mean to be callous, but when you have a pool in an urban area, this kind of thing happens sometimes. And unless it's someone important, it's a footnote in the newspaper, quickly forgotten and glossed over. At this point, I can only hope everything blows over and that justice is one day served.

CHAPTER TWO
LIFE AT COVE RIDGE

I pull my Ranger pickup into the Cove Ridge Trailer Park. There's no masking the exploits here. Whether it's shrieking, moaning, killing, singing, or screaming, we've got it all.

Beat-up cars going in and out, equipped with their latest fix.

Kids on bicycles, inches away from being mowed down by the same vehicles.

Infidelities conveniently accomplished in a waterbed on the same singlewide floor plan two lots over, either direction.

Pot-bellied men carrying glass bottles in paper sacks at dusk.

I'm not complaining, merely observing. To ask for anything more would take a move across town and double the salary. I've gotten used to this with time, but if I ever find my way out of here, I won't hesitate. Trailer after trailer, side by side, packed tightly on lots so close I can stick my hand out the window, nudge the house next to me, and hope to God I don't knock it from its crumbling cinder blocks.

Arriving home, I turn the engine off. The narrow drive-through lane has enough room for a single car and nothing more. I keep lot one-forty-three relatively tidy for a bachelor, but I can't say the same for my neighbors. Joan on one-forty-two is a forty-something chain-smoking cat lover with an affinity for cheesy snacks from mail-order catalogs. She's low maintenance, unmarried, and okay with that. Why she keeps rollers in her hair all day long, I'm unclear, but somehow it matches well with her bathrobe stained in cat piss.

Who am I to judge? I'm single, forty-something, and okay with it, too. I've never hated the idea of companionship. It's just never been a thing for me. Times change, though. And, with that in mind, I guess I just have to ride the wave.

Dave on one-forty-four is an entry-level taxidermist with more dead animals mounted to his walls than he knows what to do with and a beer drinking habit that leaves his six-by-six garden more full of crushed cans, beer branded collages, and bottle clinking windchimes than should be legal this side of the Mississippi. As for the taxidermy, we're not just talking about a couple of deer, racoons, or field mice. The guy does possums, dogs, and cats, too. Some commissioned pieces having been from the likes of Joan but remain unaccepted and unpaid. They just aren't that great. Don't get me started. People do weird things to get by when they're in a pinch. Dave's been pinching it a while.

I grab a stubby Flitz beer from the fridge, plop down in my recliner, and turn on the TV. I've grown accustomed to the occasional roach that runs down my east wall, but I don't care anymore. They never loiter, and it's rare I'm fast enough before it slips out of sight somewhere behind the wood paneling and the outer wall. There is one tonight, but I'm not getting up again. Tonight's feature, a seedy game show called *Twisted Hacks* on Channel 33. Most of the time, I change the station, but after seeing a dead man in the pool this morning, I'm a little jaded, maybe even numb, making trash TV a welcome distraction. The show's distasteful, but I can't help but watch. It's locally produced, and there's just something about the host's pompous, devil may care attitude. Nearly every element of the unlikable guy is a faux exaggeration, and I'm sure the actor playing the character is bound to be tired of the ugly blonde wig and sunglasses by the end of each episode.

As for the setup on the program, it's a simple two-camera game show with a lot of whimsical music, bright pastels, and spinning floors with three contestants rushing to answer a list of macabre questions, a timer counting them down to an unfortunate fate. There's anonymity to the program, though. Each player wears a different colored motorcycle helmet with the visor down, and they're only called by their first name.

At the episode's conclusion, scores are tallied, and each contestant receives their "Final Verdict" after a trip to the "Wheel of Doomsday".

Castle Productions, the studio responsible for *Twisted Hacks,* is known around town as the alternative to homelessness. It's something the producers regularly flaunt as if they're doing something meaningful to pour into the lesser people of the community. Maybe they are. As for their other programs, there's only two, a slasher of the week show called *Freaky Fred,* and a situational sketch comedy called *Squirrels Chasing Rabbits.* Even Dave has resorted to going on *Twisted Hacks* when he's fallen on hard times. What he blew the money on, I couldn't really say. Garbage in, garbage out.

As for me, I'm an ordinary guy with better things to do than sulk and feel sorry for myself. To do otherwise is unhealthy. I drift away for the night in my living room recliner. My bedroom's only a place for momentary escape, never extended sleep.

1969

The front door squeaks open, and dad's work boots clomp across the floor. Rounding the corner, he carries an eight-millimeter reel lifted from base beneath his left arm. He skips past mom, grabbing a cold beer from the refrigerator, and giving my brother, Denny, and I a nod to come into the garage with him.

A feeling overtakes me. I'm confident this is one of those father-son moments that I will never forget. Dad pulls out our projector from a dusty box in the corner and props it up on a pea-green table picked up from a yard sale. I haven't confirmed this, but I don't think he's allowed to have it inside, or so my parents' most recent argument leads me to believe.

There's a glimmer in his eyes today. It's rare to see him this way. Anything beyond work or politics just doesn't keep his attention. He rests his beer on the table, the bottle quickly sweating, an unsightly ring forming beneath.

Looking us both in the eyes, dad smiles as he clears his throat. "Guys, there comes a time in a man's life when he has to decide what kind of man he's going to be. A man that lives for his nation... or a man that lives for himself. There's not a right or a wrong answer, but there is a better one."

I look at Denny. We both study the blank sheetrock the projector shines upon as the old man threads the 8-millimeter reel. There's a PROPERTY OF US GOV'T tag on the side of it as it spins, making it even more official as it cues to a voiceless barrage of video clips. The soldiers in uniform, running, jumping, rolling in the dirt, lining up outside barracks, firing guns, their drill sergeants yelling. The reel flashes and flickers to the mess hall, the commissary, and the officer's club. The men on the video running through a complete gambit of emotions.

Dad narrates, "Men, there's no shame in staying home and keeping your house clean. But I'd wager that's something to do in retirement. These men, they made the right choice. The better choice. I know none of us are pleased with the Viet-Cong right now, but you know, it's... uh... an important time we're in. Think about the impact you could make."

The reel ends. Awed with excitement, I look over at Denny. His eyes are glossed over and he's uninterested.

Dad continues his speech. "I've got a variety of tires, ropes, and materials that will make our backyard a fine training ground for two able-bodied young men. I'm not going to vet this past your mother, because I feel in my heart... *this* is what you were made to do, sons. Now, make me proud!"

My vigor makes me want to spring to my feet. "Yes, sir," I yell.

We make eye contact. "There are lessons to learn in life, guys! Your mom and pop won't always be around to clean up your messes. Will they?"

My old man looks at Denny, who remains lost in thought. "Always the momma's boy, aren't you, Denny?" his voice, curt and strong as he gulps down his beer. "Unless she ain't looking..." He gives Denny a playful slap on the cheek. "Now, prove me wrong. Let's set up the backyard and make men out of you!"

CHAPTER THREE
MUSINGS OF A MAVERICK

1991

There's a fine line between the misfit and the maverick. Sometimes, it's hard to tell the difference. I've always been one to color inside the lines, pay my taxes, and lead a boring life. My... setback's part of me, and I can't change it. I just have to look forward. I'm not the kind of man to categorize everything. There are nuances. I mean, these are the kinds of things that define a person's identity, setting one apart from another, but I'm no expert in character study. I think I'm ordinary and, to be honest, that's okay with me.

As for the body in the pool, we're at twenty-four hours now, and Greenwich has already told me to move on. I don't think the incident made it in the newspaper at all. Jerry said the man was better known in Barton Hills, only an occasional visitor to Riverton. I don't think I believe him, though. I'm not saying he's a killer, but the victim probably had more to do with the hotel or another sketchy business than anyone will let on. These kinds of killings are usually meant to send messages. The question is to whom, and why?

As I start the shift, my marching orders are much the same tonight. Thankfully, the lingering traces of the man in the pool are gone. I still struggle. I see him there when he's not. Some kind of post trauma thing, I'm sure. As a precaution, Jerry had the pool drained shortly after to keep things sanitary, and it's been refilling all day with several hoses dipped in to expedite the process. I skim the top of the swimming pool, scooping the fallen leaves to the side. Leaning the pole against the fence, I drag a new cover across the water. As the moon shines across the night sky, I check my watch, 12:47AM. There's not much nightlife around here. The Bridgewater Restaurant and Bar entertains until 2AM, but it really isn't my scene.

I finish up my evening duties. The chlorine treatment should be finished by first light, and I'll check the pH. I aim for 7.3. It's delicate, but manageable in the right hands or hand, in this case.

As I'm locking the gate, an unfamiliar huddle of figures stands behind the hotel storage building. A rush of cool hits my spine. I think of yesterday's floater, and wonder when my day of reckoning will come. Will I even be missed? My eyes follow the silhouettes as they disappear and the faint whispers of their voices are washed out by traffic and crickets chirping to the sky.

Perhaps it would be a tad cut and dry for the dead man to be associated with these fellows, whoever they are. Perhaps not. There's something in the air tonight. It's different. I figure they've seen me doing my thing by the pool, so I'm not tiptoeing around to finish up, but since Greenwich hasn't mentioned them, I'm on guard. I've got to dig in a little— to get a little nosier. I carry my supplies to the building. The voices rattle off phrases in familiar rhythms just behind. I get quiet and try to listen, unannounced. Before I can make out much of the conversation, the back door to the hotel pops open and Jerry waves me in. He's flustered, seemingly unnerved by my proximity to what's going on back here.

"Sir, I wasn't expecting to see you. It's late," I call out, brushing debris from my shoulder.

"Come in, Greg. We need to talk," he says, his voice dropping to a whisper.

"Who are they?" I ask.

He raises his finger to his lips, nodding his head toward the hotel. "That's not your concern."

We go down some steps nearest the rear entrance and approach his basement office. He unlocks the door and clicks on the green banker's table lamp. Sitting down in the chair, he removes his glasses, running his fingers across his mostly slick scalp. I study his long-troubled eyes— his inability to sit still, a clear indicator our meeting's purpose isn't good. The smell of his coffee perks the room up a tad from the musty, smoky smell I'm accustomed to, but it's no match for his body odor. He's been sweating.

He sighs. "Greg, this is brand new information, and I'm still processing. So, let me just get it over with," he says, looking at something scribbled on a sheet of paper. "New business ventures leave the hotel with no choice but to relieve you of your duties, effective immediately."

I drop my head, raking my fingers across my fresh crew cut. Greenwich's beady little eyes stare me down as I catch my breath. He's struggling, too.

"I don't understand, sir," I say, a bead of sweat running down the back of my neck, my heartbeat's tempo on the rise. "What's wrong? Was it the body? Is someone pressing charges?"

"No. Not that I'm aware of. I think the board made a mistake, but my hands are tied."

"What? Why?"

"The hotel's board of investors is more concerned about parking spaces than they are a swimming pool. Keeping the pool is too much a liability. With Bridgewater just across the street and public intoxication rampant, this drowning sealed the deal. It's dollars and cents, Greg. Nothing more."

"Drowning? Sir, I told you the man didn't drown. The body was dumped."

Greenwich shakes his head. "You keep saying that, but I still don't know why. The cops think otherwise. I know you think you're an expert at this, Greg, working the pool for so many years. But leave the business stuff to me, and I'll leave *you* to you."

I squint my eyes. "I don't follow. Can't we put up higher fences? A better lock? That might help prevent this from happening again."

He shakes his head. "There is no 'again,' Greg. The body's not the primary driver. As mentioned, the parking lot is the future. We'll put a blacktop on the east side of the hotel— free parking for guests, and paid parking for city visitors that need a place to park to wine and dine. With all the revitalization around here, this is just another way to help keep things afloat in the early reopening stage. Paying for maintenance and upkeep of a swimming pool's just not a priority anymore. We'll have her filled in and sealed up for good by the end of the week." Greenwich picks up a cigar from a box on his desk and lights it, turning his head momentarily to take a drag.

I clench my fist. "Mr. Greenwich, I can handle other maintenance on the grounds, sir. My skills aren't limited to swimming pools. Or, if you need a parking lot attendant, sir..."

Greenwich blows air through his lips and sighs. "And I quote... 'Pools are my life. It's the only job I've ever had.' What am I supposed to do with you, Greg? I can't afford to pay for training on the job. Besides..."

"Besides, what?" I ask, my protest less than silent.

Greenwich leans in closer toward me. He's sweating worse than when we started. Maybe the lamp's hot, but my money's on nerves.

"Texas is a right-to-work state, Greg. I can fire you for any reason at any time. And in this case, I gave you the courtesy of telling you why. Take my word for it, it's not personal. It's just business."

I sit there, struggling not to explode.

"You may not understand this, sir, but I've given this pool twenty years. To see that evaporate for a parking lot is just... devastating. I know you have to move on and so do I."

"It's not the end of the world, Greg. With enough money, people can always put in their own pool. Don't worry. We'll give you a severance. There are other jobs to be worked in this town. Take a step into the unknown. It'll do you some good."

I look away, inhaling deeply.

This termination discussion has gone on too long, and Greenwich's inexperience is showing. "Don't you have any parting words, anything else to say or to ask of me?"

"I don't."

He blows another puff of smoke. He's clammy, probably counting down the minutes to ease up his own tension. It's an emotional thing to fire someone. "Well, good luck, Greg. I'll talk to you later."

That human, feeling part of me isn't ready to disconnect. "Is everything okay, sir? Did anything else come of the body?"

"Not really. Nothing juicy. Terrible way to die, though."

Normally, I'd put up a bigger fight, but I don't have the willpower. There are days in my life where I spoke up too soon and didn't just let things happen.

"I guess that's it, then," I say.

Greenwich nods, handing me an envelope. "Good night. Your severance is built into your paycheck."

I take it from him. I don't even have to open it to laugh at the piddly amount. As I walk to the door, I turn around. "Mr. Greenwich, those people out back, who are they?"

He looks back, stands up, and peers through the window at the abandoned tunnel running behind his office. "That's not your concern. You're no longer an employee here. Good night, Greg."

Walking out the rear entrance, I collect my thoughts. There's no one around. I approach the pickup and head home. It's an uneventful drive across town, Whitesnake on the radio to keep me company.

***

I awake in a cold sweat as the hum of the air conditioner comes to a halt and the power goes off. Eyeballing the calendar on the wall, I punch it.

Shit!

It's September 5th, and I'm behind on rent and utilities. I start moving stuff from the refrigerator to the ice chest I have staged for this scenario. Suffice it to say, this is not the first, nor the last time I'll be doing this. There's a pounding at my door, quickly followed up by another series of knocks. I open it. Will Stoltz, the Cove Ridge mobile home park manager, stands just out front in a stained wife beater and baggy blue jeans, his well past five o'clock shadow, an ever-present indicator that looking after Cove Ridge is his only livelihood.

"Preakle! You're overdue on rent. I'm not gonna warn you again."

I nod. "Yeah. I just got paid. I'll square up with you by the end of the day. I promise."

"Your promises are only as good as you prove they are, freeloader."

What a jackass. I can't stand the guy, but what do you do? He's there, a pesky fly that never leaves.

"I'll get you paid."

"Well, that's when the power and water come back on, and no sooner. If I don't have something by Friday, you're out of here."

"It won't be an issue," I reply, closing the door. I'm mad, but he's just doing his job, and I'm taking advantage like half the others around here. Who knows what favors it takes to keep *him* appeased?

I've got to do something. Look at this worthless wretch. Kick me out of here. Put me out of my misery.

I sit down. I could have explained myself, and mentioned I'd lost my job, but here's the thing, I don't want pity. For the entirety of my adult life, I've always been Greg Preakle, the one-armed pool man. I'm sure the people and kids that have seen me through the years have nicknames and stories about me. Speculations about my personal life that are far more whimsical than the truth. Or even the idea that I'm all that different. Asking for sympathy at a time like this only perpetuates more of these assumptions.

I lay the newspaper down on the end table to balance the page and peruse the classifieds. It takes some one-handed dexterity. No positions to match my skills. I get up and walk to the front door, eyeing my mailbox mounted on the porch. The communal one kept getting knocked over by drunks in pickups, so the pathetic Cove Ridge HOA concluded *this* the more optimal solution.

I grab the mail and carry it inside. Rifling through the bills, I jot down my remaining expenses on a yellow pad, comparing them with the mediocre funds to my name. As I reach the bottom of the pile, there's a promotional advertisement on a folded sheet of blue paper.

LOOKING FOR CONTESTANTS ON CUTTING EDGE GAME SHOW…
A GATEWAY TO GREATER OPPORTUNITIES.
STOP BY CASTLE PRODUCTIONS, TODAY.
MUST BE 18 OR OVER.
DAILY PAYOUT $500 PER PARTICIPANT, $10,000 PER WINNER.
1836 OAK HOLLOW LANE, RIVERTON, TEXAS.

Hmmm. I guess I am that desperate.

I head to the fridge for another stubby, carrying the flyer with me. Arriving back at my recliner, I stroke my cheeks and contemplate. I've driven past Castle

Productions for years, but never entertained the thought of involvement there. I much prefer it from the other side of the screen. It's not top-notch entertainment, nor is it looked upon favorably by the commoners in Riverton. Five hundred bucks is enough to entertain the thought in a moment of desperation— ten thousand, of course, a much greater motivator. I need money and I need it yesterday. As I drift away for the night, the stiff air and dark room remind me that it's time to get things in order, pronto.

CHAPTER FOUR
MONEY TALKS

I struggle to swallow my pride—knowing what it really takes for a man to stoop to such a low, but I don't know what else to do. There's no underlying motivator here beyond a man's pursuit to prosper himself well enough not to end up living under a bridge or begging mommy and daddy for money.

Pulling into the parking lot, I take a deep breath and climb out. The bright and multicolored signage of Castle Productions illuminates the sky, leaving me to consider what else I might do to make ends meet amidst monetary struggles.

It's all temporary, Greg, just a few minutes of foolishness.

Studying the building and its unassuming yellow bricks, I cringe. The place is uninteresting. Certainly not kept up to the standards of its Californian counterparts, but we're none the wiser in Texas. I step inside and look around. There's high vaulted ceilings, a few posters, and a sitting area. The facility's an early 1900s construction; Castle having moved in sometime in the last few years.

A lone receptionist sits in the dim lobby with a knockoff Tiffany lamp. The security lights on either side of the room reveal tired eyes and graying hair. As I approach, I note the building's considerable depth.

"Excuse me," I call out unenthusiastically, "I'm uh... I'm here to audition for a slot on Twisted Hacks."

She studies me, staring at what's left of my arm for a few seconds and takes a drag of her cigarette. "Oh, yeah, you'll do just fine, honey. We were looking for one more tonight," she says, leaning over and pulling some paperwork from a desk drawer. "I'll need you to sign some papers and we'll get you on the list. We're doing some tapings this evening. You know how this works, right?"

"Yeah, I think so."

She jabs a cigarette on her well-charred desktop. From the burn marks, it's at least the thousandth time, and no one seems to care.

"Just fill out these liability waivers and acknowledgments, and one of our production assistants will take you back to the studio. Make sure you read over it carefully. You don't want to miss the fine print."

"And just like that, win or lose, I get five hundred? What's the catch?"

She nods, her unsteady gaze, disconcerting. "You have to participate in all associated activities. As you've seen on TV, it can end messy."

I make eye contact with her a moment before replying, "I guess I'll deal with them as they come."

She looks at me and returns to a game of solitaire spread across her desk.

I continue with the paperwork. "TV's all just a bunch of smoke and mirrors, right?"

She nods. "What they get away with in there... it's..." she says, momentarily disengaging with her cards.

"It's what?" I ask, working my way through the forms, and not paying much attention. Signature after signature. Initial after initial.

"Unconscionable," she says with a whisper.

"And why's that?"

She shakes her head and bites her lip, her lack of words, the best answer.

Dropping the pen and documentation on her desk, I nod. "All finished."

She sighs. "Are you sure you want to do this? It's usually just the bums and slug suckers coming in. Forgive my saying this, but you're a little cleaner cut than the average contestant."

I purse my lips. "Slug suckers, huh? I'll take my chances."

We walk around the corner. I'm blinded by a bright yellow sign.

An obnoxious voice overwhelms the room through surrounding speakers.

"Play one... play all... play one... play all... Castle Productions Presents—*Twisted Hacks*... cable TV's bloodiest quiz show!"

The host's awful face is caked in makeup, filling a display monitor backstage—his huge white teeth, veneered and polished a shade too glossy, his maniacal laugh memorable enough to chill contestants through the ages. My predecessors approach the stage. The camera pans to the spectators in the room. They're all in black masks, faceless, voiceless, and emotionless, unless cued otherwise.

I consider my rationale for doing this. Is a half hour block on trash TV and an abysmal single-wide on a thirty-eight-by-eighteen lot worth the hassle?

I'm lost in the moment as the host's warmup monologue becomes a dull hum. There are two others waiting, both more destitute than I am. None of us can stomach sharing words as we watch the terror unfold on the screen. A person desperate enough to pay a bill in this manner has either burned every bridge to success they have left or just dark and disturbed enough that they're willing to take any risk for 10 Gs.

The host rambles through the loudspeakers like a theater flunkey better suited for a desk job in accounting. There's an applause sign mounted to the wall that lights up only when the clown makes a stupid joke. To the untrained eye, it's all macabre entertainment. As I'm standing in the next room, I wonder where the lines between fiction and reality actually blur, because from here, it's all real.

An underwhelming production assistant speaks to me and the others. "Well, this taping is just about over. It's about time for your group to go on stage... Godspeed."

I stare at the screen, watching the winner go up to the top of the stairs and slide down into a bathtub full of cash. He's donning a red motorcycle helmet. I suspect the anonymity this offers removes network or company liability for damages or injuries to guests on the show and spares the guests embarrassment from family and friends. This isn't *my* proudest moment. The waiver essentially covers everything, and the late-night cable regulations allow for a "free-for-all" considering the gratuitous nature of the violent content on the program.

The host's voice bellows with positivity. "Congratulations to tonight's winner, Johnny! He'll be taken home in a limousine with a briefcase full of cash and two lovely women. What they do after that is *their* business, not ours! Ha-ha!"

The crowd applauds, a canned laughter triggering just before. It's twice as loud through the speakers, compounded with the studio's natural acoustics and checkered tile floors.

The host's voice grows darker. "And for the losers... it's time to spin the Wheel of Doomsday!"

I watch the monitor as the wheel waits for its next revolution, its multicolored faces not so different from *Wheel of Fortune.*

"Helen. Come forward," the host orders. "Spin the Wheel of Doomsday!"

Poor Helen's had both legs amputated below the knee. She rolls across the stage in a wheelchair. Her fanny pack and misplaced accessories are complemented by a purple and black spandex number.

"Spin it, Helen. A new future's 'dead' ahead!" the host yells, his smile sickening. The camera pans to the audience, all brainwashed into the same manic delusion of terror.

I can't see her face, but beneath that motorcycle helmet I know she's second guessing her choice.

"Three... two... one... and she spins it, folks!" the host yells.

My eyes remain mystified by the allure of the spinning wheel. I haven't reviewed every fate it offers, but I'm told only one is favorable.

"It's about to stop!" the host yells, his yellow sports coat and hairpiece an ugly combination to the washed-out pastels on the surrounding walls.

The crowd continues to cheer beneath their masks. It's all so disorienting.

"Helen, you've landed on the... Meat Grinder."

They wheel her across the room and a bright light shines on the awful apparatus. Her hands hit the sides of her helmet as she squirms in her wheelchair—the crowd's reaction and applause growing louder and louder. The rhythm to it all makes me sick. I'm seconds away from choking on my own vomit.

"I guess it's time we... get things moving," the host calls out.

The camera pans to a massive ten-foot machine that resembles a meat cleaver pounding the table below it in three second increments.

"Helen, one question," the host asks, grabbing her arm and chuckling, "Left... or right?"

She pulls away, working to open the visor on her helmet with her left hand. A security guard rushes toward her, slamming her arm on the table.

"Left one it is... I hope you're a righty! Ha-ha!" the host says, his gritty voice grossly invigorated.

The rhythmic clapping of the audience doesn't stop. The bizarre emotion in the room is appalling, like a terrible nightmare with no end. Tying her wrists to the table, the crowd counts down at the cue of a lighted sign in the background. "Three, two, one..."

The cleaver drops onto Helen. Her screams muffling in the helmet as the upper part of her arm pulls away from her elbow in a clean separation. I hurl all over the chair in the makeup area. The assistant calls out to me, "Oh, gosh! Let's get you cleaned up. You guys are on next!"

"I can't do this," I say, wiping the vomit from the sides of my lips. "I want out!" I say, standing up and walking toward the door as a security guard blocks the exit.

"You signed the waiver. You're now under the employment of Castle Productions," he says gruffly, crossing his arms.

I can't see his face, he's wearing a black mask, too, just like all the rest, his only identifier, a black t-shirt that says SECURITY.

The PA raises his voice at me again as a scream from the next room echoes and the crowd cheers and applauds. "Put your helmet on, now!"

CHAPTER FIVE – TWISTED HACKS

My throat's dry, they're all watching, and I'm spinning around.

The milky purple walls wash into yellow then back to red.

The black masks everywhere.

Their voices humdrum and monotone.

The rhythm to their claps uninspired.

And the insufferable host is amped up twice as loud.

"I'm so glad we're here tonight! Aren't you?" he yells. The question's not directed toward the contestants. It's definitely aimed at the audience. I'm quickly concluding their cheers are never sincere. I've heard of such a thing as a paid audience, but I've never seen it before. I'm not sure what to think of this one. There are plenty of people that get way too into blood and guts, so a live show might not be all that intense to them. They're all desensitized, maybe deranged.

I'm in the red helmet. There's no definitive correlation to success as far as I can tell, but there is a counter at the back of the studio that shows the number of victories under each helmet throughout the show's past four seasons.

RED - 138

BLUE - 125

GREEN – 71

Maybe I am having a stroke of luck. I don't want to jump to conclusions, though.

Dizzy, desperate, and dumb, this is my last resort. My brain's scrambled like a batch of stale eggs, the spinning floor stops, and I lock eyes with the host. They never call him a name. In fact, his stupid nametag just reads, THE HOST. That's all we get.

There's a familiarity behind the theatrics. It's just too masked and distorted for me to know why I feel this way.

I study the room. Spaced out in different spots and in the shadows stands the Meat Cleaver, the Atomizer, the Scalpatron, the Dentalizer, and the Fire Poker. They're all grisly. They're all gruesome. And we're all here, wondering what the hell's about to happen to us.

At this moment, my heart's ready to pound straight out my forty-one-year-old chest. My skin and ribcage aren't enough to hold it back. Somewhere deep within, a switch flips and my nose goes to the grindstone. I want to win. I need to win. And I can't care so much. These people are here for the same reason as me, and if a phrase like "take no prisoners" ever applies, it's right now, as we all hope to God that no injury's actually inflicted. The sheer number of waivers I just signed leaves me unconvinced.

Blue helmet's in the hot seat. The question's in motion. If she doesn't hit the buzzer and answer within ten seconds, it's fair game to me and green. We need all the help we can get. As for this show, it's too hard to tell the difference between what is real and what is special effects. I don't know, and that scares me.

Up until now, I've never taken things all that literally, but everyone else seems to struggle. They don't always get dark irony, that comedic punch, that quickness on the draw. That little part in the back of your mind when someone picks on you because they like you but for a split second, you think they hate you. And that's when I realize, I'm more an oddball than I want to be, doing all I can to fit the mold of the All-American Man, less my lower right arm. Some mold that would be.

Blue gets the question wrong, spins the wheel, and ends up at the Scalpatron. May God bless the poor hag. From what I saw backstage, she already had patchy hair. That compounded with her age, drug abuse, and lifestyle tells me she'll soon be a goner.

I answer the questions as my body and mind move into an unknown fourth gear and adrenaline kicks in. I usually idle between second and third, never really going pedal to the metal. It's in everyone's best interest that I don't. You can thank my parents for my learning to avoid it.

Growing up, I hated watching them heat up and lash out at each other. You know what I'm talking about. It's that moment when shit hits the fan and the only thing keeping mom from running a butcher knife through dad's heart is the fact he's hidden it right before. We're always talking about hindsight. Thank God for foresight, right? Their coping skills were about as refined as hyperactive monkeys, and I'm no less immune. This problem's hereditary.

Like I mentioned before, idling between second and third gear is the best part of Greg, the normal part. I'm comfortable, agreeable, and mildly likable. Anything beyond that, and I'm right on par with the whackjob hosting this shitshow.

I'm sorry, I'm just not ready to lose another limb. And no, I didn't lose the first one here, in case you were wondering.

Question. Answer. Applause. Question. Answer. Laugh. Timer buzzes and I'm on my way down from the top of the studio on the slippery slide and into a bathtub of cash. It's stupid, but I won. No more fourth gear. Blue's been scalped. Green's been atomized. And Red takes home victory number 139. The host tries to pull me backstage and chat as we wrap the episode, but I'm too sick to stay.

CHAPTER SIX
VICTORY LAP

I head home, my mind more fractured and disturbed than before. I look at the briefcase in the seat next to me— full of money, who knows where it came from? Somehow, I did, in fact, win. I'm not celebrating, though. Ten thousand bucks spends fast, but at a minimum, it buys me some time. I make my way across town, struggling to lose sight of the spinning Wheel of Doomsday and the unfortunate fates of my fellow contestants. The production crew has reassured me, they're all okay, but I was ten feet away, and it all looked a little too real. Green and blue don't have a return ticket to *Twisted Hacks*. I can assure you of that.

There's virtually no credibility to anyone trying to snitch out the studio, either. Some contestants go on the show repeatedly to nurse bad habits. The city's disproportionate amount of people missing limbs and with distorted appearances are attributed to injuries in Vietnam and Korea, not some second-rate cable program.

I make it into Cove Ridge. A black Towncar sits next to my house parked— its brake lights reflecting crimson on the side of my kitchen window. I'm unsure whether to drive on by or go in knowing that all the neighbors are witness to my unannounced guest. I circle around several lots further down, and pull in behind the car, just out front of Dave's house. I wave at him and approach the car. The darkly tinted windows tell me nothing of the driver or passengers inside. The window rolls down three inches. I can only see the brim of a black hat.

An edgy, raspy voice speaks from behind it. "Mr. Preakle, congratulations on your victory tonight. Fork over nine thousand dollars before we make a scene."

My heart sinks. I'm not packing heat, nor do I have a means to defend myself from the unknown harasser.

"I don't understand. I was told this was mine at the close of the show, no strings attached."

"No limbs attached, ha-ha," the voice says, sneering. "Don't turn this zip code into a crime scene, Mr. Preakle. Hand over the money, and we'll leave you alone."

I look back. Dave sits on his porch sipping a beer as if he's taking in a gritty, twisted thriller on Showtime. There's no light on, but I can still see his silhouetted shadow. Before my harasser can say anymore, Dave pulls a pistol from beneath his shirt, shooting toward the rear window of the vehicle and shattering the glass. The driver spews obscenities as he races away.

My heart pounds as an unexpected thirst overwhelms me. How I could sweat so much in so short a time is beyond me.

"Don't worry, neighbor," he calls out, motioning me toward him. "I got you covered."

I can only muse as I walk over. Neighbors being in each other's business gets a bad rap, but sometimes we intervene for the good of our fellow man.

"What was that?" I ask. "Man, am I glad you were here. How can I ever repay you?"

Dave smiles, clearly not as worked up as I am. He's a lot more proud of the inebriated crackshot he made than he is concerned of my harasser. "I'll take a fresh box of nine-millimeter rounds and a six-pack, and we'll call it square."

"Done."

Joan and Stolz approach from opposite sides. We congregate on Dave's porch beneath the moonlight.

"What the hell was that about, Preakle?" Stolz asks, studying me. "Are you mixed up with the wrong crowd or what? I took you as a loner type."

"That car was out there for twenty minutes, Greg," Joan says, a cigarette in her hand. "I've been watching them through my window. I just figured it was a relative, so I didn't pay them any mind. I'm sorry."

"Preakle, not a word to the cops," Stolz says. "The last thing we need in Cove Ridge are a bunch of red and blues."

I peer around. A few others are looking out their mini blinds as a row of porch lights come on in relative succession.

"Just tell 'em a transformer blew over here and we'll call it a night," Stolz says, starting to walk away.

"What are the odds one of them won't call it in, anyway?" I ask.

"What were they after, Preakle?"

"Someone else found out it was payday for me and was trying to rob me," I reply.

"Do you have any debts beyond what you owe me?" Stolz asks.

I shake my head. "None. I'm a paycheck to paycheck guy, but that doesn't mean I'm en route to debtor's prison."

"Good! Goodnight, Preakle," Stolz says, walking away, more quickly dismissive of the incident than I would have expected. Joan follows a little behind, going her own way.

Dave cocks his head back toward him and unfolds a lawn chair next to his. "Have a cold one with me, Greg. You're not gonna rest easy tonight without unpacking some things first."

I sit down. He pulls a beer from his Styrofoam cooler and hands it to me.

"You're right," I say. "It's been a rough day."

"What's going on in your life, Greg? How are things?" he asks, his words slurred, his voice deep and pronounced.

"Not great. I got fired, whored myself across the airwaves for cash, and almost got robbed, all within twenty-four hours."

Dave nods, perching his lips out. "Yeah. These things happen. I heard what the driver said, Greg. You're a little richer today. Aren't you?"

"Yeah. I went on *Twisted Hacks* and won ten grand," I say, my pride deflated.

"Wow, another victor, living right next to me. I'm proud of you, neighbor!"

"Stolz was going to evict me. I had to do something. I just can't help but wonder, though."

"Wonder what?" Dave asks.

"They fired me at the hotel 'cause I found a dead body out there in the pool. Now, I've got guys harassing me over here. Am I jumping to conclusions? It's hard not to feel targeted at this point. I know coincidences can happen, though. Tell me I'm not going paranoid."

Dave nods, his hand resting on the broken side of his lawn chair.

"Could be, buddy. Or, you just pissed off the goddess of chance with the good fortune and now you're paying her back."

I laugh. "As a drunken musing man, you've got some interesting theories, neighbor."

Dave chuckles. I know that he means well. He's just trying to ease my mind for the night and deflect the stress of the incident.

"What do I do, man? Do I call the cops?" I ask. "Should I get them a little more involved here? I know I won't win any popularity contests with Stolz, but I don't really care at this point."

He grins. "That's up to you. I don't have all the answers. You know something, though? I do have something else that might help you."

"What's that?" I ask.

"With you being out of work and everything, I know someone, Greg. An old buddy of mine that can use a guy like you."

"Like me? What do you mean?" I ask, sipping on my beer.

"Unemployed, but willing to work."

I nod. "Okay, I'll go with that. What's he do?"

Dave gulps his cold one, popping open another. "Well, his business card says he's in education, but I think he dabbles in a bit of everything— a jack of many trades, a master of none. I'll call him in the morning and let you know what I find out."

"Alright. Well, I owe you a lot, Dave. Thanks," I say, extending my left hand to shake his. His grip's firm.

Dave smiles. "Yep. His methods and style are a bit... unorthodox. So, don't be surprised if your interview is, too."

"Alright, thanks. Like I said, I need a job. I'll speak to you in the morning."

Dave reaches under his chair, pulling out a pistol. "Here, take this nine-millimeter, and keep it nearby. I'll just be lounging out here, anyhow. Don't worry, I'll keep a watch on your place."

I try to wave the gun away. I'm not surprised. Dave's the kind of guy that keeps one nearby just 'cause he can. Accepting it seems inappropriate, though. Dave and I are cordial enough, but I've seen too many episodes of *The People's Court* where lent possessions end up turning into small claims court fiascos.

"Thanks, Dave. I don't think I need it. I've got you here if I need anything, right?"

"I insist," he says. "I've got a dozen others. Just take it."

I'm not going to fight him. "Alright, then. You are some kind of saint, neighbor."

"Nope. I'm definitely a sinner."

CHAPTER SEVEN
NEIGHBORS AND NIGHT TERRORS

My night is plagued with traumatic images of my short stint in the Castle Productions studio.

I'm standing there on the stage in a stupid, oversized green polo shirt and a dated pair of bell bottom blue jeans. My hair looks like crap, too.

The host's voice booms through the speakers as I spin. "A dead woman's found on the ground in her beach home with a cassette deck and a .44 magnum. When the sheriff's department arrives, they immediately play back the tape to review the prospective evidence. On it, the woman says, 'Yes, it is my day to meet Jesus,' and then the gun pops. The cops rule it as a homicide instead of a suicide. Why?"

I look out at the audience and then back at the host as I spin in circles, the room's circular shape further disorienting me.

"Because..."

"5... 4... 3..." the host and crowd chant in an eerily scripted unison.

"Because the tape was rewound," I say. "If it were a suicide, the cops would have had to rewind it first."

"Very good! You're an astute observer, Gregory." the host says, smiling widely. He grabs my shoulder and holds on for a second, almost like we're old friends. I signed up as Greg, not Gregory. My mother was the only one that could call me that.

***

I wake to a pounding at the front door, wiping my eyes and getting up slowly to see the source of the ruckus.

"Hey, neighbor," I say, peering through the screen door at Dave.

"Hello, 'mister soon to be gainfully employed!'" he says with a smile. I pop the door open and he sits down.

"What?"

Dave grins. "I had a chat with my friend, and he says he thinks he has a position for you."

"Wow," I reply, still a little slower than I'd like to be. "That's great news."

"Just have to ace your interview."

"When does he want to meet?"

"I told him you were free tomorrow morning. His name's John Fatts. You'll meet him at Richland Lake near the marina."

"Richland Lake? Is this a marina gig? I thought you said he was in education."

Dave shrugs. "Yeah. He likes to take the boat out and cast the line a while. Told me the best way for two men to talk and get to know each other better is when they're preoccupied with their hands, not sitting across a table from each other in crappy designer suits."

"I get that," I reply, chuckling. "Alright, I'll meet him there, then."

"He told me to tell you to make sure you dress to fish— not your Sunday best."

"Alright. I owe you big time, buddy!"

"I reckon you do. Don't forget the twelve pack and the two boxes of ammo."

"I thought it was a six-pack and one box."

"Don't go cheap on me, Greg," he says, smiling. "You know where to find me."

As he walks away, I pull the screen door closed and sit back down. Working to gather my thoughts, I realize that in all of last night's chaos and after a few cold ones next door, I completely forgot about the money. I panic, flinging the screen door to the house open and hustling to the truck. Without that money, I'm only a few hours from panhandling on a street corner with an eviction notice. Joan waves at me before she takes a drag, as melancholy as always. I wave back, but don't say anything. Peering through the window, I see my winnings waiting for me and breathe a sigh of relief. I unlock the truck and grab the briefcase. Thank God it's unscathed. I bring it inside, placing it in my unpowered freezer. That's the last place someone would look for it, right?

CHAPTER EIGHT
UNCONVENTIONAL INTERVIEW

My commute to Richland Lake is uneventful. A boring drive with little to carry on about beyond my Twisted Sister cassette. Arriving at the marina, I notice another small pickup parked on the edge of the lot and a large bald man sitting just inside. He waves at me, getting out sprier than I'd expect a fifty-something to do. He has a slight limp and a well-endowed gut to carry. As I climb out of the truck, he approaches.

"Gregory Preakle?" he calls out.

I nod. "John Fatts?"

"Right on the money!" he says, his warm handshake and southern drawl rendering him immediately likable. "I've been looking for a morning like this to cast my line with another for a good while. Thanks for meeting me," he says. "Follow me over here. We'll take the Tarkano out into the middle of this swamp and have us a good old time. You take the lines and I'll grab the cooler."

They're in the back of his truck. We both lean over the edge and scoop them out.

"Can't say I've ever interviewed for a job in a boat before," I declare as we walk toward the dock.

"Nor have I conducted one," Fatts replies with a grin. "It'll be good for both of us. You look like you could use some sunshine. Any friend of Dave Levett is a friend of mine."

After launching the boat into the water, we run through the normal introductory pleasantries and a few generic interview questions as the sun pierces through an otherwise hazy sky.

A quiet morning seems just what I need. Somewhere in the back of Mr. Fatts' mind, he must hope his candy apple colored fishing boat attracts fish like a red muleta does a bull. Cracking open beers like old friends, we let the rod and reel do most the talking and the calm of nature surrounds us.

Our conversations have volleyed a bit this morning. Fatts has domineered the bulk of them, though. I'm just nodding my head to improve chances at gainful employment. The job he's hiring me for is at my alma mater, West Riverton High School. Coincidentally, West Riverton houses the district's only swimming pool, all courtesy of some wealthy philanthropist's desire for their snot-nosed grandkid to be a state champion swimmer.

Fatts slowly reels his lure back in, breaking an extended silence. "Atmosphere, Greg. There's just something about two guys casting rods in peace and quiet that can't be beat."

I nod. "You're right. My pop would take me and my brother out on the water as a kid and we'd catch and release. Mom wasn't much a fish eater."

"Your pop, huh? You guys have much to do with each other anymore?"

I'm mystified by the question. It's an overreach, but in hopes of not jeopardizing employment, I play it down. "I guess so."

"I'm sorry. No intent to intrude, just a fellow man checking up on another. These relationships matter a lot more than most of us want to admit well into our adulthood."

I curl my lip and ponder. "We're amicable when we need to be. Things have just been different since... since we lost my mother."

"Oh? I'm sorry for your loss. Was it recent?"

"Well, not exactly. We lost my brother in combat about eighteen years ago and it's just never been the same after that."

"I'm sorry to hear that," Fatts says, reeling his lure a little closer to the boat. "I'm sure he was an honorable man, too."

"He might have been. Nineteen's too young. He was hardly a man."

"Vietnam, I take it?" Fatts asks, pulling up his sleeve and showing a military tattoo. *173rd Airborne Brigade.*

"Thank you for your service," I say.

He nods. "It was a hell of a war. Sometimes, the kids would walk out with bombs strapped to 'em," his voice drops out, his eyes glossing over. "You can't unsee it. It's deep-rooted. I'm sorry. Now I'm getting too personal."

"It's okay, sir."

Fatts waves me away. "It was a confusing time for all of us. I've changed a lot through the years, tapped into my lighter side. Everyone can use a laugh now and then. It cures the worst right out of us."

"Hmm... Interesting thought. My escapes... a couple of cold ones and some hair metal. Otherwise, it's a mundane life, and that works well for me."

"Mundane, huh?" Fatts says, his reply a little underwhelming. "I think the job at the school will give you a change of perspective. Transform you. We've got some characters over there; they'll have you fuming one second and loving them the next."

"No offense, Mr. Fatts, but mopping floors and taking out garbage hardly sounds like an opportunity for transformation."

Fatts nods. "Whatever you say. We'll just see about that."

I pin my emotions, grateful for the opportunity. "Thank you, sir."

He turns his head toward me. "It's nothing at all. You have a nice attitude and an impressive philosophy on work ethic. There's only been one problem with our interview."

"What's that?"

"The fish just aren't biting today," he says.

"Nope, they sure aren't. Let's change things up," I reply, dipping my hand into the minnow and bait bucket.

"Here, let me thread that on the line for you," he says. "That can't be easy."

"Be my guest." I inhale deeply as he gets my line ready. "Hey, listen. I appreciate all you're doing for me. I've been resting on my laurels a little too long. The school will be a nice change of pace."

Fatts smiles. "It will be. I guaran-damn-tee it. Not only that, you'll also have our swimming pool to treat, now, Mr. Preakle... Hey!" He pulls at the rod as something catches on, his smile, big and wide.

"You got something?" I ask, my eyes lighting up.

He nods, his teeth gritted together as he reels it in. "It seems like it." Pulling it up, he fights resistance on the line. Emerging from the water, the gleam of the morning sun reflects upon the scales of a beautiful flip-flopping bass. "Well, what do you know? I'll bet it's a ten pounder. You don't see that every day, do you?"

"We might have dinner after all," I say, adjusting my cap and scratching my head.

Fatts jams the fish into the ice bucket. "It'll thrill Lynette I actually caught something. She's always working and traveling, barely makes any time to cook. I'm just too lazy to bother with it. She and I are on the outs. It's a seasonal thing. She'll snap out of it soon enough," he says.

I study the rippling sheet of water beneath, wondering if I should enable the talk any further. "Oh, and why's that?"

"Uncontrolled impulses, Greg. Too many of 'em." Fatts says, his face souring. He pulls up at the front of his waders. "It's my fault, too. I hire these beautiful women, and then they just gravitate toward me. I guess I'm just what you call a charmer."

I reach into the minnow pail to hand him more bait for the line, accidentally pulling out a slug.

"Oh, sorry. I didn't see the slug. I'm guessing you want the minnow?"

"You know the Tarks catch on better?" he mumbles, sipping on his brew.

"The... what?" I ask.

"The Tark slugs. What you just pulled out from the bottom of the pail. The fish go crazy for them."

"If that's the case, then why haven't..." I pause. "What are you doing with these, anyhow?" I ask, my inebriation removing my normal inhibitions.

He sticks his hand out. "Hand that one to me. Will ya?"

I hand it over. The diplomacy in our morning fades away as I watch Fatts bite the tail off the unexpecting critter and spit it in the water, holding the mostly brown antennaed creature near his mouth. "I usually do this behind closed doors, but what the hell? If we're gonna be family, I've got to let the secrets out as they come," he says.

"Do what?" I ask, unsure of his bizarre actions.

"Count to three and suck," he says, laughing to himself and inhaling the innards of the slug.

I'm inches from upchucking my morning granola over the side of the boat.

"No chlorinated pH in this guy," he says, a glowing glimmer in his eyes, "but I've always thought wet's better than dry." He cocks his head to the sky. His voice bellows into a jovial laugh. "Oh, man. The clouds in the sky are bluer. The fish are greener. And everything seems right in the world," he says, chuckling aloud. "Mmm... mmm... that rush, it'll change your life!"

I adjust my cap, forcing a more casual reply than deserved. "You said something about chlorinated pH? You've got my interest piqued having cleaned pools for twenty years."

"At home, I'll dip the slugs in the swimming pool to get them moving faster. Let me tell you something, Greg, it's a rush and a half."

I nod. "You ingest pool water?" I ask, sipping on the stale beer and reeling my pole back in empty-handed. "No offense. But how in the world did you figure *that* out?"

He agrees. "It's a fair question. I was drunk. One night I was out by the pool at my place and kicked a little pail of the suckers into the water by mistake right after the pool man had treated it with the chlorine. Boy, howdy, you should've seen how fast they moved in that water. It was like nothing I'd ever seen before. I tried one after the fact and it was like a double hit in one suck."

I shake my head. I've always been a little apathetic to the slug-sucking phenomenon. It's been a problem around here for a while now about like any other drug, but seeing someone of Mr. Fatts' stature in education doing so this openly is unexpected. A principal addicted to this sort of thing; it just seems so out of place.

Stolz, on the other hand, he'd be more who I'd expect to catch with one. Yeah. Stolz would definitely be a slug sucker.

I think of the kids at the school. The staff working for Fatts. I'm a little bothered. Is it really my place to ask? Sure, why not?

"Mr. Fatts, can I ask you something?"

"Yeah, shoot."

"What implored you to join the slug sucking crowd? You don't strike me as the 'hippie, earth-loving' type."

"This is not just any slug, Greg," he says, swigging his beer. "There's a lot of potential here."

I nod. "I see you're quite the optimist for them. Why is that?"

Fatts shrugs, brown goo seeping out the sides of his neck. I haven't been around enough slug-suckers to know what the norms are but I'm assuming this a known side-effect. "It's the euphoria. The rush. That adventure of going into the unknown with all holds unbarred. Leaving that light on one second longer to get that extra bit of awareness." He laughs, looking away as we cruise across the water, the swelling waves trailing just behind.

"Hmmm."

He reaches into the bucket and tries to hand me a Tark. "You ready for one?"

"No, thanks. I don't think I can handle that today. I never got into anything that... edgy."

He waves me away, dipping the critter into the lake water for two seconds. He pulls it out before biting the tip of its tail off, spitting, and inhaling it. "Mmm. Perspective, Greggy. Perspective. Life's too short to keep a stick up your ass." His face becomes more flushed as he lets out another sigh of satisfaction.

I can't help but think this an odd philosophy for someone in educational administration, but I need a job. Bonkers or not, this guy is my lifeline right now.

Before I can muster words, Fatts squints his eyes at me. "I see you looking at me differently," he says. "Here I go, trying to share an intimate moment with you, and *this* is how you respond?"

"I'm not sure I follow, sir. I'm looking forward to the job."

"Sure, you are. I'm not making you uncomfortable? You look at me like you're repulsed, like I'm second class. Do you look at the old lady next door differently because she smokes? Do you judge your brother because he drinks? People cope with stress in different ways, Greg. Sometimes for me, it's just a quiet afternoon pick me up. And without the side effects of hard liquor or smoke inhalation, I might add. It's all natural, anyhow," he says.

I gulp as I speak my mind. "Natural... with an extra helping of pool water?"

"Yes." His quick reply tells me I've stepped out of bounds.

"I'm sorry, sir. I'm just feeling a little... sunbaked. Whether a man sucks a slug, drinks a beer, or smokes a cigarette now and then is between them and God. Who am I to say otherwise?"

Fatts' eyes are bloodshot as he speaks, "I hope you really do feel that way, Preakle. Dave told me good things, and I expect them out of you."

"I won't let you down."

"I think it's about time we call it a day," he says, starting the boat and cruising us across the water. As we approach the marina, he mellows out. "We're both roasted now, anyhow, and I hate sunscreen. Makes my skin all oily, and I can't stand it." Killing the engine and climbing out of the Tarkano, Fatts ties it up beneath the cover.

"I'll see you tomorrow," he says, slurring his words. "We'll iron out specifics in my office and get you moving. Your first day... Start at noon-time. The shift runs until 9pm with a one-hour lunch."

I nod. "Sounds good."

"Oh, and one more thing, I'll need to keep you on a 1099 as a cash employee," he says. "It's, uh... only temporary while you learn the ropes. Five an hour for starters and we'll stair-step you up as time goes on. No benefits yet, I'm afraid. Hopefully Uncle Sam can cover you in light of your... condition."

"Okay. That's fair. As for Uncle Sam, it's complicated. I'll take my chances."

"Enjoy the rest of your day. Our custodian, Will Hoblitz, will show you the ropes when you arrive. He's a bit of a grumbler, but you'll get used to him or learn to tune him out quick. Just between us, I don't care what you do in your spare time as long as you make me look good."

"Alright. Yeah. I remember Hoblitz. He's been at the school for ages. Even since I was a student there. Take care," I say, approaching the pickup.

"Oh, yeah? I hadn't even thought about that," Fatts says. "See you later."

CHAPTER NINE
TAKE A LOAD OFF

I pull into Cove Ridge, realizing I've gotten across town quickly without a lot of effort or thought. I keep playing the less than predictable meeting with Mr. Fatts over and over in my head. From his unexpected antics, my stint at the school may be a shorter-term gig than I expected. As I climb out of the pickup, Dave sits on the porch next door with a new stuffed calico cat that's misshapen frame makes me wonder how the guy ever makes a living.

"Hey, neighbor," he calls out, popping open another beer. "How'd it go?"

"It was good. Mr. Fatts is an... interesting fellow," I say, biting my lower lip. "I start tomorrow."

"Hear, hear," he says, raising his beer in the air. "I'll drink to that. To neighbors, and to connections!"

"Thanks, Dave. I owe you."

"No problem. It's all good. I've got a running tab. We'll square up when we square up."

"Take care. I need a shower," I say, heading into the house.

"Good night, neighbor."

I've already planned the evening out. I need some time alone to decompress. I don't have worthwhile hobbies or collections like Dave or Joan, but I occasionally like a good thriller film and stopped by the video rental shop on my way home.

The power's back on with a little help from my recent "victory" and severance check. I load David Cronenberg's *Videodrome* into the VCR. As the coming features play on the television, I go into the kitchen to make myself a turkey sandwich, grab a handful of potato chips, and throw them onto a small plate. My kitchen calendar shows Dali's *Persistence of Memory,* better known to the less artsy as "the melting clock." I mark tomorrow's date in black marker ink.

FIRST DAY AT NEW JOB!

It doesn't take long before I've inhaled the sandwich and I'm drifting away as James Woods runs across the screen some kind of antihero in a world more unusual than my own.

1969

After a night of indiscretion with some friends near the city pool, my brother Denny and I come inside our house, passing through the living room. We're several hours past curfew and the television's still on. It appears to be a repeat of the evening news.

"A report on a troubling new fad in from downtown Riverton... More from the field in a moment..."

Dad's already turned in for the night, but mom's in the kitchen washing dishes and waiting for us. I motion to Denny to go on to his room. Mom will undoubtedly smell the chlorine and alcohol in a heartbeat, and I'm not doing very well at keeping my kid brother's nose clean. Denny's a "straight A" student. A few more drunken benders like this one, and he's on a fast track for the "C list" right next to me.

I move toward my bedroom feeling bothered, not only from our poor choices, but of my forthcoming lifestyle change. Slipping my shoes off, I turn the shower on. Before I can get in, mom's voice rattles at me from down the hall.

"Gregory, is that you? Turn that shower off and come in here. I want you to see this."

"Alright. Alright. I'm coming," I say, turning the water off and moving through our mostly barren wood paneled hallway.

"Hurry!" she says.

Arriving in the room, I'm wasted and worse for wear. Mom studies me, certainly noticing my inability to look her straight in the eyes, the odor of illicit activities lingering. She points at the television as the commercial break ends.

The anchor stacks papers on the newsroom desk and clears his throat. "Authorities say they're unclear where the body came from, or how it came to grow so deformed and decayed in such a short amount of time, but one thing's for certain. Trouble lurks in Riverton."

The news report cuts from a caution taped crime scene to the coroner, briefly speaking on the matter. "I've dealt with druggies, crooks, and psycho grannies, but I've never seen a death quite like this one. We'll be running some more tests to conclude the cause of death. The brown goo coming from the victim's skin is what troubles me most. Our testing gives us no conclusive data."

The news report goes back to the studio. "John, actually, what we're hearing from residents of the former Oak Hollow Hotel is that he's yet another victim to a new, rising addiction problem that we have here in Riverton. Look at this interview shot earlier in the day..."

An older homeless woman is featured on camera next to the news anchor in a trench coat. The hotel stands in the background, decaying and dilapidating. "Yeah. That was Stu. He was into strange things... I mean... the things only the poor and desperate do. I don't even... I shouldn't..."

"Shouldn't what?" the anchor asks, moving the microphone closer to the woman.

"I shouldn't talk about it. Sometimes... us poor folks have got to make ends meet in different ways to... cope with the stress... you know?"

"No. I don't. What do you mean?"

"I shouldn't say nothin' else," she says, her sunken posture and malnourishment apparent.

"Ma'am, please go on," the reporter coerces.

"Well, a few of us, we, uh... got a little mixed up into something we don't quite understand. Down there in that 'ol tunnel under the hotel, we found these slugs. We call them Tarkies... Tark slugs. Poor man's crank. You get what I'm sayin'?"

"No, I don't," the reporter says.

"Well, seein's how it ain't illegal or nothin', I don't guess there's no trouble in showing you. I got a couple."

The report flashes to the anchor sitting in the studio. "We want to warn our viewers that the next segment may be a bit troubling for younger audiences. Discretion is advised..."

As the scene goes back to the field, the woman pulls a slug from her pocket. "Here's a Tarkie right here. You just bite the tail off and suck it. It's easy. You want one?"

"Why would I?" the news anchor asks, his nose crinkling.

"It's a high... a rush. You know, we can't afford the good stuff, so we've found somethin' even better. It makes your skin crawl a little, turns it a little slimy if you take it too far, but otherwise, it's harmless." The woman rakes a drop of goo from the top of her head onto the ground.

"Harmless? What about... Stu? The dead man that was found."

The woman breathes deeply through her nose as she replies, "The slugs wouldn't kill him. He probably just took his other drug habit one step too far."

"How's that?" the anchor asks.

"I don't know. I ain't his sponsor. Why should I care?"

The anchor nods. "Alright, then. So, tell me this, how did *you* come to the conclusion to... suck slugs?"

"Desperation... you know? Escargot's a thing... right? It ain't so different. We were munchin' and the next thing we knew, we were on cloud nine. Why don't you try?"

The anchor hesitates as he looks toward the camera. "Well, I'm on the clock. I'll let you do the honors."

"Too good for it, huh? Figures..." the woman says, biting the tail off, spitting it to the ground, and sucking.

"Good god in heaven," my mother calls out as she gasps.

I can't help but let out a grin. There isn't much that rattles mom, so this is a rare treat.

The woman on the TV continues, "Yeah. That's what I'm talkin' about. Mmm! You mind if I sit down a minute? You know, to take a second to clear my head?"

The segment cuts back to the studio. "Tark slugs... I don't know what to say about that," the co-host says. "This is troubling."

"Not only is it troubling, it's downright peculiar. We're out of time for tonight. Join us next time on Riverton NightWatch."

My mom turns the television off. "Gregory, I need to ask you something."

"Okay. What is it?"

Mom strokes the sides of her cheeks. "I know you and your friends hang out over by that old hotel. I hope *you* aren't into that..."

"Into what?"

She lights a cigarette and takes a drag. "Sucking slugs."

"No, mom, but now, every teenager in Riverton knows the cheap way to get high and that lady just told them where to find it."

"I guess it's a good thing you're leaving tomorrow. Your father and I have just got to keep Denny away from it for three more years 'til he's out from under our roof."

"He flies pretty straight, mom. I wouldn't worry about it," I lie, a growing concern lurking within.

She leans in and hugs me. I'm sure more for a motherly inspection than any sort of affection. "I can smell it, Gregory. You better get yourself sobered up before morning. Don't worry, I won't say anything to your father."

"Yeah, I'll get cleaned up. Good night, ma."

"Good night."

CHAPTER TEN
NEW JOB

1991

Arriving in a mostly full parking lot, I study the red bricked facility known as West Riverton High School without enthusiasm. My four years here as a student back in the 60s were more than I needed and naturally, I don't think many fancy returning to the same place they smoked their first joint, had their second heartbreak, or received their third or fourth ass kicking. Nonetheless, here I am. The style of the building, a testament to tens of thousands just like it: Paint peeling on the window frames. Two years overdue a good power wash. Overgrown hedges. And wads of chewing gum jammed everywhere imaginable. I could go on, but I won't.

I head toward the building. A door opens on the far side of school's lower level. That's when the scratchy Yankee accent of Will Hoblitz, the longtime school custodian, comes through loud and clear. I'm sure he's had his fair share of students, teachers, and staff through the years that he'd rather forget, including me. Despite years in the area, the fellow's failed to adopt the slower-paced southern charm most of us have by proxy. Instead, he carries a shorter fuse and a lot of hostility to the world around him.

"Get yourself over here, son," he commands in a screechy voice.

"Okay," I call out, approaching him. I'm not going to push buttons from the beginning. I'm here to learn, and to remain employed.

I study Hoblitz. His face is older, but his waistline remains the same. In fact, I think the goof's probably still wearing the same uniform he wore when I was a student over twenty years ago. It wouldn't surprise me if he sleeps in it, too. I struggle not to feel sorry for him, thinking back to how we made fun of him when he mopped the floor, his crooked gait, and the growing bald spot beneath the swooping swirl of hair he combed across the back. And now, here *I* am... I'm that guy—one arm less than he, I might add.

There's a look in his body language that tells me he's two or three years overdue on his retirement, but still needing the paycheck to make ends meet. He stares at my arm for a second before motioning with his head to follow him. The fellow leaves me wondering if the bum leg we used to make fun of is in fact, a prosthetic, but I'm not about to lift his pant leg to check.

"We'll get you setup and I'll show you around," he says, pulling out a comb from his back pocket and slicking what's left of his hair. "The job's not rocket science, son."

I do my best to remain respectful. I'm straighter laced these days. For some of us, adulthood certainly changes our perspective.

"Thank you, sir."

"I'll spare you the details on what to do," he says. "You've got a working brain, don't ya? The task lists are over there, and everything's spelled out simple enough that a dog could read it."

"Well, thanks. You know something? I was a student here before," I say.

He nods, pulling out a tool from his cluttered steel gray work cabinet. "It might surprise you, but I remember you, son."

"Do you really?" I ask, raising my eyebrows.

"Of course... Never forget a kid that comes through these doors."

"Really?" I reply, slightly flattered.

He chuckles, slapping me on the back. "Hell no. I'm just kidding. Fried too many brain cells on the booze in the break room in my early days to keep up as well as I should. As long as you weren't destroying school property or breaking into my work area, I wouldn't remember you. You never did that now, did ya?"

"Of course not. I was a pretty good kid," I say. "I remember you, sir. And I'm thankful for what you did to take care of this place for all these years. I know it's bound to be unappreciated, but so essential!"

"Well, ain't that a sappy line of shit? Let's get you to work, kiss ass!"

He presents the work area to me. The workshop is wide open, with all kinds of tools and cleaning supplies lining the walls. There are also storage cabinets, a wall of posters of pin-up girls, soda fountain and bar memorabilia, and a huge "Don't say no to the USO" sign.

"Were you in the USO, sir?"

He shakes his head, rifling with the keys in his pocket. "Can't say I was. And enough with the sir's, Will or Hoblitz is fine. As for the sign, it's been up longer than I've been around. Never been much the caring or hospitable type, nor have I given a rat's ass about décor around here. Take it all down and make it your own. Fatts doesn't care about what the work area looks like. I don't guess you need much more a tour of this hellhole. Do ya? You were stuck here plenty long—carrying out your four-year government sentence, right?"

"That's a smart way to look at it," I reply. "How about showing me around a little? Just the basics."

"Son, time is of the essence," he says. "I'm ready to retire my scrawny ass and live the rest of my life doing more of what I enjoy and less of this crap."

"What do you enjoy?"

"Not wasting my time, and that's what this feels like."

I sigh. I'm never going to please this guy. "Okay. I'll follow you around for a while, if you don't mind."

Hoblitz hands me a timecard. "Go punch this over there, and I'll take you up to the attic to change out the air filters. They're a little tricky."

"Yeah. Never went up there before," I mutter.

"Of course you didn't. I never let anyone up there—kept it padlocked a lot of years, just a big open space for me to leave the little piss ants that crossed me to rot in their shackles," he says, maintaining a poker face.

We walk up the stairwell on the far east end of the campus and Hoblitz pulls out the key to the padlock. His hands are wobbly as he struggles to thread it into the slot.

"Oh, for crying out loud!" he says, slamming his fist on the door. "You do it. My hands are too shaky." He hands me the key. "It's that gold one with the number on the side."

We pop the door open and go in, the smell of death coming over us.

"Holy momma from Tijuana!" he yells. "Who died?"

Hoblitz shines his large Maglite across the large attic area—a glorified wasteland for the West Riverton Theater Department. There are piles of leftover prom decorations dating all the way back to Ike in here.

"I think the better question is... what?" I say, trying to lighten the old codger's mood. "Unless those piss ants in shackles you mentioned weren't a joke..." We approach the air conditioning handlers. "When's the last time you changed out these air filters?"

"Between you and me, son. It's been about five years. It hurts my old back too much to be lunging that way to get in there and change it out."

"Couldn't you have just gotten someone else to help you?"

He sighs, reaching for his back as we walk across the room, finding his way to the light switch. The room brightens in strategic spots across the long, vaulted ceiling. "I can't be looking weak. They'd fire my old ass for something like that. We'll just drop the filter right here. You can pitch the old one over there behind those old Halloween decorations. I don't give a damn, and neither should you. This job ain't never been appreciated right."

Trading out the old filter, I find a dead raccoon on top of one of the attic air handlers.

"Oh, gawd, son. There's the smell right there," Hoblitz says. "I'll bring up a couple of sacks, and we'll get this little home-wrecker out of here. I don't want to cause a scene, though. You understand? We'll leave it here until everyone clears out of the school after hours."

"I'd have figured it would have been more decomposed by now, as rank as the thing is," I say, pinching at my nose.

"Yeah," he says, nodding. "Probably one of the damn kids around here pulling a prank."

"I thought you said none of them ever got in here."

"Well, sometimes I'll hear a creak and a groan. I figure, now and then, the kids sneak in through the ceiling tiles above the auditorium stage—dangerous, but not impossible. I ain't gonna say nothing, though. Let kids be kids."

Walking across the attic and near the stairwell, I notice another door.

"How about what's in there? Anything worth mentioning?"

"Just storage. What I don't see won't bother me. What you don't see won't bother you."

I study his face. "Strange answer."

"Not really. I'm just short on time and not in the mood for twenty questions with a one-armed brown noser."

"Excuse me?" I reply, agitated with the cranky killjoy.

"I'm sorry. I'm gonna go, son. I'll be here at the school first thing in the morning. If you want to follow me around tomorrow, meet me in the basement work area at 0900. You can work your way through the checklist tonight. There's plenty to do."

I nod. "Okay. I'll plan to see you then. Your shift's already over by 12:30? Any other suggestions for me before you go?"

"My shift ends when I say it does," he says, scowling. "Give Mr. Fatts space to do his thing and ignore his vices. Everything else will fall in line just fine."

"So much for training on the job," I mumble.

"Walk around the school. Keep your self looking busy, empty the garbage bins, that kind of stuff. That'll be good enough for today."

***

It's been a few hours. I've worked my way through most of the task list. As I finish my rounds through the building, I walk into the classroom just above the basement. A pyramid is sketched out on a chalkboard with a bunch of dollar signs and arrows pointing from top to bottom. I erase the board, turn out the lights, and empty the garbage. A bit later, I move toward the administration wing of the school. The light in Principal Fatts' office is on. Two men are chatting softly on the other side.

"This is the future in our hands," Fatts says behind the door. "If channeled correctly, imagine the potential if we can... if we can... expand."

Eventually I knock, having tidied everything in and around the outer administration office.

"Come in," Fatts says.

"Yes, sir," I reply. "Just here to take out the trash for the evening."

As I come into the room, he slides some paperwork just out of sight and beneath a pile of books. There's a familiar face sitting in the chair just across from him.

"Greg, this is a longtime friend of mine and the school, Dr..."

As we make eye contact, I remember our family doctor and my mother's longtime therapist.

"Carl Hicks," I interrupt.

"Greg Preakle," he says, standing up and shaking hands with me. "It's good to see you."

"Likewise. What brings you here to the school?"

"Well," Fatts interrupts, "Dr. Hicks is here to do some consulting and serve as a sort of de facto counselor and medical expert when I need him for the students. I'm short a nurse and a counselor right now, Preakle. I got a little too involved with them earlier in the year and had to let them go for... personal reasons."

Dr. Hicks grins and pats me on the shoulder. "Do you ever feel you're living in a soap opera here, Greg? I'm still scratching my head how this guy keeps a job. Ha-ha."

"Don't push your luck, Doc," Fatts says. "Contracted hires don't have to stay contracted. Do they?"

"Have a good night, gentlemen. It was nice to see you again, Dr. Hicks. Take care," I say, walking out of the room.

It's a little odd. I can only piece together what's in front of me here, but having an MD on retainer seems like overkill in a high school. I've got mixed feelings on Dr. Hicks. He's been loved and respected by my family for a lot of years, but there's only two of the four of us left. Some caregiver *he* was. I guess I'll keep a watch on things. That nosy part of me's kicking in about now, and something about all of this just isn't adding up. I know I've got to be careful how I ask questions, though, and to whom.

1979

I stare mother's physician and psychiatrist, Dr. Carl Hicks, in the eyes closely as he places her hand into mine. She's been at the hospital a week now and seems to be stabilizing after her most recent episode.

"It's been a rough few days," he says, "but I think we've got her meds adjusted to where she can get back out there and take a stab at life again. What do you say, Brenda?"

Mom's face is pale, her frame much frailer than the sturdy woman I grew up with. As she musters up the strength to speak, I look her in the eyes and smile.

"I'm feeling a little better, Gregory. I need fresh air. This place chokes the life out of all of us."

"Remember, Brenda, stick to the regimented schedule on the medicine for it to be most effective. You can't skip, and you can't overload, either. It's just like a vitamin or anything else. Take it as directed, and you'll see the results in due time."

After Dr. Hicks takes us to the checkout counter, we sign a few papers to honor mom's request for discharge and move toward the exit. I keep hold of her hand as we walk down a depressing hallway of other minds trapped in perpetual chaos. Climbing on the elevator, we exit the behavioral and psychiatric floor, and I give her a hug on the ride down. "I love you, mom."

"I love you," she replies. "And I love Denny. I need my Denny," she says, tears streaming down her face.

I'm helpless. I can't tell her to 'pull it together,' and I can't bring him back. As we climb into the car and drive across town, there's not much discussion, only the swishing and swashing of the windshield wipers, and the occasional honks of the other cars following us down the interstate from point A to point B. Truth is, I've been planning to move out from under her roof for a while, but I haven't told her yet. Her recent breakdown has slowed down my plans. The divorce doesn't help. Dad's gone for good, and I think they're both better off this way.

After we've been home a few hours, I've made dinner, and the television's on as a much-needed distraction. I've taken a quick break to tidy some things up in mom's room before she goes to bed for the night. As I prep the blanket and pillows, commotion erupts in the next room as mom taps, punches, and stomps all over the house— always in increments of three.

Coming back in the room to check on her, I see mom standing in the kitchen in her nightgown, the lights off, a pair of scissors in hand, and her breath elevated. Lunging toward the kitchen table, she jabs at its wood, chipping at it a piece at a time. I turn the light on and approach her.

CHIP. CHIP. CHIP.

Her face is carved up with chunks of skin missing, her blood dripping onto the floor.

"Mom? Mom? What's going on?"

"It's all your fault, Gregory," she says, swiping at her hair with the scissors and lopping uneven pieces of it onto the brown carpet beneath us.

"Is that better? Huh? Is that better?" she says, charging toward me.

"He never would have gone if it hadn't been for *you*! He just *had* to please your father. And where did he end up?"

I shake my head as a tear streams down my cheek. Peering down at my necklace, I imagine Denny in combat. The poor kid blown to smithereens. I sigh. "Mom, you know that's not fair."

"Nope. Nope. Nope!" she yells, kicking at the wall. "Dr. Hicks tells me to hammer it out in three's... to quiet all these impure thoughts. It's not working, Greg," she says, a tear streaming down her bloody cheek.

"Mom, you're not well," I say. "You need help."

"After your father ditched me, I just... haven't been coping well. Abandoning his sweet woman in her time of need. I swear I could just..."

I interrupt her. "Mom, you and dad have been passing ships in the night a long time, now. It was inevitable."

"I'll show you inevitable!" she yells, moving toward her wrist with the sharpened scissors.

I rip them out of her hand, wrapping my arm around her to subdue her in the moment of frustration. "Mom, mom! Stop this before you..."

"He's gone... He's gone..." she says, her blood and tears smearing all over her gown and my once-starched shirt. "Look at you... you're going to be late for work. Get out of here, Gregory!" her cracking voice, uneven and harsh.

My shirt's a mess. I can't in good conscience leave her this way. I want to honor her wishes, though. Perhaps some time on her own will be good for her.

"I'm going to change," I say calmly, trying my best not to add drama to the scene.

Mom screams, swiping the scissors toward me again. "Just throw it out. I ruined it! There's no washing me off, Greg. Your old mom's done a lot of bleeding for you. A whole lot! And for your brother..." she says, dropping to the floor and continuing to cry. "I don't think you'll ever understand."

I dab a tear from her cheek. "Mom, I'll take a sick day. We can work this out."

"They're just going to put me in a padded room or load me up with more pills. I don't want that!"

I drop to my knees, embracing her tightly and hoping to calm her, stroking my hand against hers.

"If you could hear how loud my thoughts are screaming at me now, Greg, you would understand!"

I rub my hand across the back of my neck to alleviate a growing tension. "I have them, too, mom. Every day I wake up, I think of my arm and... I have them, too. The dead and dismembered piece of me, missing— my head blaring at maximum volume to 'come home.' We'll get you help, mom, I swear."

She scoffs. "Gah! Just one empty promise after another— just like your father. Who knows what floozy he was with when I was gone?"

"Mom, no one! You know, he was nothing but faithful to you. The two of you had your differences, but don't you remember? He lectured us for years, 'marriage is a sacred covenant.'"

"A sacred covenant that can be broken!" she yells. "I'm forever violated! Go ahead and get preachy with me. It won't work, Greg! Not anymore. I'm not buying it. I can't. No, no. I won't!" she says, her escalating voice making my heart palpitate. "Any man drowning their sorrows in that much work must be 'putting out' for another woman."

"That's not fair to you... or to dad... or to Denny. Dad's a man of dignity and worth, and he deserves that respect."

"You don't understand, Greg," she says, squeezing my nub. "It was a façade. Behind closed doors, I was a slave... a slave! He never loved me. All these unmet expectations..." she yells, punching my arm.

I shove her hand away. "I'm not comfortable talking about this anymore. Save it for a professional," I reply, immediate regret coming over me.

"Of course, you're not. It's a matter that shouldn't concern you, but who else can I turn to?"

CHAPTER ELEVEN
BEER DRINKIN' AND HELL RAISIN'

1991

After closing out my shift, I drive home. The night sky's washed out by city lights. My car speakers blare a familiar riff from Ratt.

I'm lost, really lost. I mean, my reality's rushing into a nightmare.

The dead man in the pool.

Fatts' affinity for Tark slugs.

The jerk-offs trying to rip me off the other night immediately after I win.

Or, Castle Productions is about to go under, and they're the ones harassing me.

Who knows? One thing's for certain, I can't keep floating by here. This rollercoaster of madness has to be taking me somewhere, and I've got to be sure I'm the one in control. Sometimes, I just can't, though. I teeter totter every day in insecurities. The only thing I've got going for me now is the fact that I'm aware.

I pull into the driveway about 10PM, slowly turning my volume down. I've probably irritated a few neighbors, but this is the closest I usually get to the wild side. Dave's outside, sitting on his porch. The crickets sing to the sky. I wave at him and prepare to head inside when he motions me over.

"Hey, neighbor," he calls out softly, his usual nightly brew next to a row of five empties. "Haven't seen any Towncars floating around here lately. I guess you're in the clear?"

"I don't know, Dave. I guess no news is good news... until it's not. What's going on with you?"

"I'm not the one with the new job, Greg. You tell me what's new."

I walk up the steps onto his porch.

"Take a seat," he says, handing me a cold one.

"I'm pretty beat," I say. "All in a hard day's work."

"You got that school gig figured out like the back of your hand yet?"

"I don't know," I reply. "I've only got one, and I know that one pretty well."

"I'm sorry. Didn't mean nothing by that."

"It's all good. The other janitor's kicking my ass, but otherwise it's straightforward."

"Why's that?"

"He's just a grouch," I mutter, sipping my beer. "I don't think it's personal."

"It usually isn't. How's John?"

I ponder on the question. I weigh out my options. Diplomacy or honesty?

"He's alright. I'm keeping him happy enough. He's paying me."

"Yeah?"

"Yeah. It's been good. I mean, it's not every man's dream to mop the floor of his high school."

"Life's work. And work's life. We do what we have to," Dave says, opening up another beer.

"Listen, I know you and Fatts are friends, but he's got some interesting habits."

"Yeah?"

"Yeah."

"Such as?"

"Well, he sucks slugs for one. He's got MD's on the payroll. And, it seems like he struggles to keep a professional distance between himself and his staff. That's a hard lead to follow, man."

"Aww, Greg. Don't be such a prude. I know Fatts is an acquired taste. He means well, though. If you work hard for him, he'll take care of you," he says, chugging his drink.

I nod, sipping on mine. "I guess. I've probably said too much. Like I said, he's paying me, and that should be enough for me to shut up and do my job."

"It's alright, man. Fatts and I are old buddies, but we do what most old buddies do."

"What's that?"

"Look past each other's flaws."

"Yeah, I guess you're right," I say.

"Don't feel you have to if you're not comfortable, neighbor, but I've always been curious..."

"About what? My arm?"

"Yeah. I don't think you ever told me how it happened."

"Alright, fine... For posterity's sake, I'll set the tone. It's 1969. I'm nineteen. It's the end of week eight in basic training and I'm growing well accustomed to the norms and expectations of the drill sarge. I'm in the best shape of my life, primed and ready to pass my PT drill. I've got a leg up on the competition, too. I remember one morning the guy barreling into the barracks, yelling in his usual morning vernacular.

'Good morning, shit for brains! It's your day to prove you're ready for combat. Get your miserable butts outside, now!'

'Yes, sir,' we groan.

'At ease. Meet out front of the barracks at 0500. When the sun rises, we'll get things moving. Are you ready for it, gentlemen?!'

'Yes, sir!' we all shout.

'I can't hear you,' his scratchy voice yells. 'Are you ready for it, gentlemen?'

'Yes, sir!' we shout even louder.

'That's better, monkeys. I'll see you in ten minutes.'

'Yes, sir,' we yell in unison."

Dave interrupts, chuckling aloud, "Go on, I'm enjoying your theatrical side."

"Several of us make a beeline for the showers for a quick rinse and get suited up in our gear. I won't bore you with the details. The things some of these fellows do to get themselves in order to start the day are far from tasteful. After a few minutes, I move toward the front of the barracks, stepping outside and lining up out front with the others.

The drill sarge yells, 'Let's take a quick one-mile warmup to get the blood flowing down to those shriveled up hind parts!'

The dirt path beneath is easy to follow and well worn, our shoe prints having dug into the earth after days and days of running and no rain for weeks. There's that pronounced smell of perspiration, not only on myself, but on the others jogging nearest me. I turn around and notice one of the bigger fellows struggling just behind to keep up as his gut bounces up and down. We're all convinced he'll at least make it for combat support personnel because he's worked his ass off all along.

The big fellow and a few others go through the PT drill. The rest of us are all watching, and each waiting anxiously for our turn. We'll need to low crawl, do the horizontal ladders, complete the dodge, run, and jump, the grenade throw, the man carry, and run a mile to be deemed 'combat ready.'

I'm on the course now. We've done the low crawl and the adrenaline's pumping. The big fellow utters a swear word in the air as he completes his time on the ladder challenge, and I'm on deck. I didn't think I'd ever hear the drill sarge cheer a man on, but we were all doing that for this guy. That brotherly camaraderie sticks with you from the get-go. You've survived eight weeks of hell together, and this is the day to prove yourself.

It's my turn.

The commanding officer's voice yells, 'Go!'

I leap into the air, feverishly grabbing one bar to the next like a child at recess, racing across the warm metal bars as two others complete the exercise to my right and left. It's the longest twenty feet of my life. The hooting and hollering from the rest are just what we need to coax us forward. Three bars left... two... one...

'Stop!' he commands.

I drop from the nine-foot perch. A bird flies toward me and as I try to stick the landing, I lose my footing and collapse on my elbow. As I hit the ground, it shatters, and I eat dirt. The others laugh a moment and then stop when the drill sarge screams at them to shut up.

My world goes black.

Before I know it, I'm in the surgical wing of the Army's nearest medical center. My arm's in some kind of sling contraption, and I'm fighting pain like I've never felt before.

A heavyset nurse calls out to me from behind a cart, 'Good to see you awake, Mr. Preakle. Bad news, I'm afraid. The osteomyelitis in your right arm is out of hand. You won't be deploying anytime soon.'

I'm in a medicated haze as I struggle to speak. 'Well, am I going to need surgery?'

'Surgery may be on the table, but the outlook is bleak, I'm afraid,' she replies. 'You landed on your arm exactly the wrong way. I'd say you were screwed over by a demon on the PT course or somethin'. I've never seen this severe an injury on the horizontal ladder drill before. Not even the heavy boys. It's usually just the legs. You'll be lucky if you're ever normal again.'

That stupid nurse never had a bedside manners course. That's for damn sure.

My emotions take me over in the moment, and I don't know what else to do. My dad always said his boys would cry tears of steel, but I'll be honest, there was no steel here. Just a worthless and pitiful whimper, better suited for a middle school girls locker room, than a grown man completing basic training. The nurse's voice grows hollow as she continues to speak, and I stare at the ceiling, losing myself in a swirl of feelings. The life I've planned will never be the same. As the nurse leaves the room, I lift the pillow from beneath my head, smother myself, and scream. It's hopeless. It's the damnedest thing, Dave. That phrase runs through my head over and over, but it translates so differently now. 'You'll be lucky if you're ever normal again... normal again.'"

I look over at Dave. He's dozed off in the chair for the night. I realize I've taken myself a little too far into the moment, drifting away from Dave, and rendering my story's effect from dull to duller.

I pat him on the shoulder. "Sweet dreams, Dave. God'll leave the light on for you."

CHAPTER TWELVE
DAD

Today's shift has been difficult. I need a break from the school. I've just coasted along through the day, my mind in a different gear than my body. I regularly struggle with nightmares as they collide with significant dates or anniversaries of events, and today was no exception. It's just one of those days where the feelings hit me in the soft spot, and I need some time to clear the air. I'm taking my evening lunch break, opting for a quiet drive across town to see dad.

I'll admit, I've come a little unhinged seeing a dead guy. I've tried to tuck it away, but it's a traumatic thing. The image burns itself deep into your mind's eye and there's no reprieve.

I pull up to dad's place—his perfect house.

The grass is lush—his trees shaped and manicured.

The picket fence, white and painted.

The home itself, immaculate as ever.

Every last shutter on the place is squeaky clean as the late afternoon sun hits it.

It's a bit of a commute to spend a lunch hour over here because I only get about twenty-five minutes on top of the trek each way, but that's usually all we need. Dad's a man of few words, but it doesn't take much for us to get the point across in our brief discussions. Besides, I'm always "interrupting" something. The man's kept perpetually busy since retirement—busier, in fact.

I slide the key from beneath the mat and let myself into the house. He's not much for answering the door when he's working and never seems bothered by my unannounced visits. I just didn't imagine it would be quite this way.

Mom, dead and gone. Dad, alone and single. And Denny, a distant fading memory. And me, picking up what's left of this shattered family every chance I can.

I walk through into the back room— the place where he does wood working and carpentry as a retirement hobby. I knock on the door. He's tapping and chiseling on something, the soft voices of Sonny and Cher in the background. What can I say? The old man's a bit of an enigma.

"Hey, dad. It's Greg."

"Come in," he grovels as a sander runs loudly.

Walking into the room, I wave. He's building a rocking chair.

"Oak," he says, slapping it on the side and turning the sander off.

"I figured as much."

"What brings you to my neck of the woods?" he asks, wiping dust from the chair.

"It's been four years since mom... well, you know. I just thought you might want someone to talk to. I don't know how much dates stick with you, but they do with me. I think it would do us some good to chat, to remember better times."

He looks up at me. His eyes never glossing over, the look on his face never changing, but a million words and years of hurt gushing just the same.

"We don't have to talk about that if you don't want to," I say. "I've been working over at West Riverton High."

"Oh?" he says. His eyes solemn, his steady hands, something to admire.

"Yeah. I'm finally getting settled in."

"I never thought we'd get you to leave that pool job. I heard about the dead man out there the other day," he says.

"Really? It didn't make the news."

"Yeah," he says, hesitating. "I picked it up on the police scanner."

"You could have called me, dad. Checked on me... You know, do what fathers should do."

"What good what have it done, Greg? It doesn't take a lot of words, son. We're... on different wavelengths. I don't resent you for it. I hope you don't resent *me* for it."

I do. Somehow, I mask it, though. It keeps the peace, taking our threadbare relationship forward year after year. We're all that's left in this family. So much potential, and so little action.

I shake my head. "You know, you could act excited for me... actually stop what you're doing for a minute and celebrate that I've made a big change."

"Greg, I'm just not that great at this kind of stuff, son. I love you, and I'm proud of you. I just don't know what else to say, or how."

"Well, I'm still going to be around a pool, anyhow. I used that as my angle in."

He nods. "Hmm... forever the Pool Man. Aren't you, son? I wonder what Denny would be doing if he were with us."

I sigh. It's always back to Denny. I pin back the hard feelings and find words.

"Probably a career man like you, dad," I say, patting him on the shoulder. "Once army, always army, right?"

"Well, for most of us," he says, staring me down a moment as he tests the rocker.

"You know good and well that's what I wanted, and I know that's what you wanted for me. I didn't ask for this."

He wedges the lower part of the rocker into the connecting piece for the front, wobbling it back and forth. "Yeah. Sometimes I just wonder... what life would be like..."

"Me, too, dad. Me, too."

I never blame him for musing this way. It hurts, but it's his way of coping.

"Death happens... and life goes on," he says stoically.

I nod. "Yeah. I guess it does."

"You know, the one thing I wish I would have done sooner was make a greater effort to appreciate the people around me," he says.

"I know what you mean."

I'm thankful for any attempt from dad to connect with me or give advice at this point. He's a man with lots of answers, but rarely shows it. I don't think he's intentionally withholding. It's just his way—with me and with everyone else.

"Well, I've got to run. I'm sorry to interrupt."

Dad lifts a finger. "About your mom, I... uh... I think about her, son. I just felt like there was nothing I could do to help those last few years."

I nod, excusing myself. A tear runs down my cheek as I pull out of the driveway, trying not to be sappy or emotional about "anniversary day." Mom exited the world the same day Denny did, fourteen years later. They say long-term damage fades away in times of loss—that people heal. Mom just withered away.

On my way out from dad's, the patter of the rain hits the rooftop of the Ranger in a beautiful rhythm, its windshield wipers moving back and forth, my mind drifting away to when it all unraveled.

1973

Dad's Buick is parked outside the house much earlier than expected. I go inside. He and mom are having dinner. They've had their difficulties but seem agreeable lately. I keep thinking tomorrow's the day I'll get out from under their roof, but the free rent and home-cooked meals seem to be keeping me around indefinitely. Before I can greet them, the phone rings.

"I'll get it," mom calls out. She attentively listens to the garbled voice on the other line. Something's wrong. Her face loses color as she drops the phone and collapses to the floor. Tears streaming as she struggles to find her words. Dad and I approach.

"Honey, are you okay?" my father asks, an uncommon concern in his eyes. He moves toward her.

As we make eye contact, I know what the call's about before she utters another word. "Mom, what is it?"

My eyes turn glassy.

"It's your brother... he's... he's been killed."

It's a surreal moment as I struggle to find emotion. Somehow, I always knew one of us would be dead younger than we should be. I just never pictured it quite this way.

"My boy dead at the hands of the Viet-Cong!" my father yells. "Damn them all to hell!" he screams, slamming his fist through the sheetrock.

The next day arrives, and I'm lost in an unshakable haze as I process the loss of my kid brother— nineteen, dead, and gone. I'm surprised mom has found the willpower to cook, but perhaps the distraction is just what she needs to escape the tragedy. The smell of the house resembles a perfect southern cooked dinner and our television blares with the evening news report as dad reclines in his favorite brown chair. Despite the emotional distance between us in the last couple of years, I am convinced she's the finest cook in the area. The table's set with fried chicken, mashed potatoes, and green beans. This meal's a bit of an unexpected rule around here on Tuesday nights.

A Bel Air pulls up in the driveway outside, and there's a tap at the door. My father greets a man dressed in military garb and invites him inside. He introduces himself as the Officer in Charge (OIC) and of his return to the US after a series of fatalities plagued his platoon, one of which included Denny.

The OIC waves at me solemnly, continuing to speak to my parents. The words feel hollow, like he's quoting a script, rather than recounting information. I struggle to fathom how much harder it probably is for my folks. You love your brother. You *love* your son.

I tune into the conversation a moment as the OIC continues. "We were out there just like any other day— hoping and praying that we'd get the call to leave. A lot of days, machine gun fire was our wake-up call. Sometimes, an explosion, and then screams and yells as men drop to the ground and meet their maker. Sometimes, Denny and I would look each other in the eye and just smile, because that's all we could do to keep positive. Despite the best of our nation's intentions, there was little we could do to change fate."

My father stares the young officer down as the man chews. Dad is rarely insensitive, but in this case, he's overbearing. His attention drifts back to the television.

Mom looks over at him, shaking her head.

"I'm sorry," she says. "Mr. Preakle's not much for conversation."

My dad's gravelly voice interrupts. "I can speak for myself, Brenda. Thank you."

My mother never challenges him, instead opting to punish him in her own passive aggressive way amidst a growing grief.

The OIC chomps on his chicken leg, his table manners a tad improper. My mother's twitching in frustration as the guy talks with his mouth full. "Your son was a good soldier. He didn't deserve to go out that way. I have something for you, though. If it's okay with you, I'd like to give it to your other son."

He pulls out a necklace with dog tags and a vial and hands them to me. "In that vial is an ounce of Denny's blood. We mixed it with alcohol to preserve it. It might seem odd to keep it so close, but I saw this practice abroad and thought it might make it more personal since most of his body was... not transportable."

A tear goes down my cheek as I take the necklace. "Thanks," I reply. "I always thought I would be the one going across the pond."

The OIC nods.

My father speaks, "Soldier, thank you for the update." There's something strangely diplomatic about dad's reply. I think mom's picked up on it, too. When you see that much death, I guess it just becomes like clockwork.

The OIC gets up from the table, extending his hand to shake my father's as he returns a weak squeeze. The soldier looks at me and studies my nub. "I'm sorry for your loss."

"I'll miss him," I reply.

He nods. "We'll do the ceremony with honors for your son at the Riverton North cemetery. Denny was a hell of a guy," the OIC says, excusing himself out. "And, thanks for dinner and for your hospitality."

As I peer out the window, the Bel Air drives away, our lives forever changed.

CHAPTER THIRTEEN
ONCE A BULLY...

1991

I guess I'm adjusting to the job. I get to the school around lunch hour. Of course, I can start the day eating in the lounge with the teachers, but I imagine my being there is more a burden than it is a help. I don't always have much that's meaningful to contribute. It's probably not all that appreciated, anyway. Good gracious, I'm sounding as cranky as Hoblitz. Maybe it's the damn uniform. Shit. There I go again.

A former classmate of mine, and the varsity boys' basketball coach, Rick Simmons, approaches me as I clean the glass on one of the vending machines. His wiry and stringy hair is his most defining quality. I don't bother to turn around. Simmons was always more an annoyance than a friend. After walking up right behind me, he blows his whistle, I'm sure hoping to startle me. We're forever two guys crossing paths and never quite clicking. I ignore him. He's one of those overbearing people that will always be around in my life whether I want him there or not.

Senior year, '69, I remember a bus ride from Barton Hills. The coach took us by the hamburger stand after we won our basketball game, and Simmons, being the goof off he was overdid it. Next thing I knew my uniform was covered in a half-digested burger. Lovely.

Fast forward a few years, 1974ish time frame, post amputation, he swung by the house with a gift, a new guitar. What was I gonna do with that? Seriously. I never worked up the courage to say anything. Maybe he was an ass, or he really *was* that clueless. I'll give him the benefit of the doubt.

I remember a few years ago, before renovations; he and his family lived in the apartments next to the pool, my pool. I would do my treatments and he'd occasionally try to toss a beer out the window from five floors up. It never ended well, usually just a beer can spraying everywhere and a bunch of kids near the pool laughing. They finally moved out of the joint, and I had a reprieve, until now. He's back in my life... again. So, I've just got to deal with it.

"Hey, pal," he says, resting his sweaty hand on my shoulder and studying the contents of the vending machine. I aim the glass cleaner bottle at him, pushing his hand away.

"Hey," I mutter. "Keep your mitts to yourself."

"Oh, Preakle. I'm just glad to see you, bud. Lots of floors to mop, garbage to empty, craps to flush. Ha-ha."

"You'd know plenty about that. Wouldn't you?" I reply, continuing to clean around the break room.

He moves closer, sticking his nose inches away from me, his coffee breath, and chipmunk teeth a great disservice to the both of us. Dropping his change in the vending machine, he keys in a request for a Snickers bar, smudging a hand across the glass.

"See you around, Preakle." He walks away, his tube socks and mid-rise shorts revealing his grubby "chicken" legs.

I refrain from getting frustrated with the glass. He's not worth the time. Besides, I've got too many people watching, and I'm still trying to cast a positive impression. I walk out of the lounge, go down the hall past rows of lockers, students, and dozens of wadded up paper balls and airplanes, and move on into the cafeteria.

The last group of students rotates through their lunch session. As I scrub each of the tables, I keep hearing them chuckle when I bend over. Reaching behind my back, I find a piece of paper taped to me that says, "Crap Scrubber." Apparently, Coach Simmons is still a ninth grader, and no other staff member had the heart to tell me. I tear it off, crumple it, and toss it into the garbage. As I work up and down the tables, cleaning each one with a wet tarry cloth, a mohawk headed chump wobbles back and forth on his cafeteria seat, trying to break it loose from the table it's attached to. I walk over.

"Kid, can't you respect things around here a little better? Don't become a statistic..."

"What?!" he says, his eyes widening, his stupid mohawk, an obvious violation to school dress code.

"You know what..." I say. "That's enough!"

Mohawk flicks me off. There's certainly an advantage to the second shift. A good chunk of my working hours are after these punks are long gone, and I'm okay with that. I walk away, heading into the serving line. The chef in the kitchen offers me a plate of food. "It's on the house," he says. "My treat. Extra seasoning on this one."

"Don't mind if I do," I reply, taking the tray out and grabbing a milk carton. "Thanks."

I sit down at a table and enjoy my lunch for a moment. Picking up the salt and pepper shakers to accent the potatoes, the salt lid comes loose and spills everywhere. I slam my fist. I'm not typically one to get my buttons pushed that easily, but I guess it's just going to be one of those days.

Mohawk and the other students around him burst into laughter. "What a gimpy loser," he says. The other kids laugh. I can't help but think of what Hoblitz has felt all these years.

"I hope you threw some salt over your left shoulder," I mutter, walking away.

"What's that supposed to mean?" Mohawk asks, his voice cracking.

I ignore him. My heart rate's elevated. Time to get out of here before I do something I regret.

"Is that a threat? Are you threatening me?" he chides.

I shake my head and stand up, my dignity still in my back pocket. One day, taking the higher road might pay off. Or, at least, I can hope it does.

Some nerve on this kid. A huddle of supervising teachers and volunteers are chattering and pointing, probably about me. I walk out of the cafeteria, moving toward the ground floor work closet. Yeah, an escape is just what I need, a little catnap. I've snatched a chair from one of the classrooms. I lock the door and flick the light out, propping my feet on the sink area and drifting to sleep for a few minutes.

1969

They argue at a volume I hate to remember, my ears still ringing. I don't know what my old man's done, but mom's chewed him up and spit him out at least half a dozen times with Denny and I in earshot, and swearing every curse we've ever heard in at least two or three different languages.

"You can get your sorry self out of here, then," she yells. "I hope it's worth it!"

Dad shakes his head. "You don't understand, honey. It was never like that."

"Like what?"

"So, you're saying you did..." her voice, rattling like a pack of pissed-off rattlesnakes.

"No. I didn't say that," he says. "It was all a misunderstanding."

"A misunderstanding you took too far?!" she screams, flinging one of their anniversary plates off the kitchen table toward dad, its blue glass breaking into dozens of pieces.

"Out!" she yells, slamming her fist on the kitchen table.

1991

I slide out of the broom closet and back into the hallway as evening breaks and haven't seemed to be missed. Making my way toward the basement, I notice Dr. Hicks going into a classroom at the far end. I find it odd that he's at the school after hours. I carry on with a few duties that will allow me to move a little closer to the classroom to see what he's up to without additional scrutiny. Approaching the room he's entered, the lights go out, and there's only a purple glow coming from within. I peek through the window and observe him moving some items along the far wall. I tap on the door.

Clearly thrown off by my appearance, Dr. Hicks comes to the door and flicks the lights on.

"Hello, Greg. I thought you were done for the night. I hadn't seen you around in a while."

"Uh... yeah, I had some other errands to tend to and supplies to stock up on. What are you up to? What's the glow over there?"

"Oh, it's just a light on one of the terrariums. Coach Simmons keeps them on overnight."

"Why do you think that is?" I ask.

"I think he's just a little unnerved by the dark."

"Why did you turn the lights out?"

"That's not your concern," he says.

"Well, it is after hours, sir. You being on premises at this time of the night is already unexpected, so it is my concern."

"Greg, Mr. Fatts and I have an arrangement. My current position often requires me to work normal business hours at the hospital. This is the only time I have to catch up on school projects."

"I thought you were here as a consultant for medical and counseling," I say.

"I am," he says.

"Well, a lot of good you're doing here at this hour," I say, my tone becoming more confrontational than it probably should.

"Greg, I've got several things under wraps right now, okay? Some of them are related to what Fatts told you I'm here for, and others are for separate endeavors."

"Endeavors that involve the school?"

"In a manner of speaking," he says, picking up a briefcase. "I've got to get going, Greg. I'll see you around."

I turn out the lights to the classroom. Walking out of the room together, we move into the hallway. As Dr. Hicks walks toward the exit, I wave. "Good night," I call out, my phony pleasantness apparent. I'm a little miffed, but more than that, I'm curious.

What's this guy doing in here at obscure hours?

Why the secrecy?

I carry on with my duties. Finishing up in the administration wing, I peek out the window of Fatts' office, watching him drive away several minutes later. I rifle around a few of the drawers. There are hints of his weaknesses planted everywhere, but on his desk, just beneath a demo life science textbook, I find a list.

Names.

Amounts.

A crude balance sheet of sorts. No further detail what it might be for.

Most of the names are unfamiliar— then I see Simmons, Hoblitz, a few other staff members. Some on the list have asterisks next to them, no amounts yet. I keep working my way down. And then, that's when I see it. Greg Preakle, asterisked and flagged. As I turn the page to check the next sheet, I see the lights come on in the outer office and quickly revert to cleaning the blinds. I flick the lights and step out. It's Mindy, Fatts' receptionist. We haven't gotten acquainted yet, but I'm flattered that she already knows my name.

"Hey, Greg. I'm sorry to barge in so late," she says. "I forgot my house keys."

"No problem. Have a good night. I'll see you tomorrow," I say, walking out into the hall. She excuses herself, and I'm on my own again.

Every part of me wants to go back in there and get a better grasp on what I was looking at, but I can't afford to get caught. Who knows what I'm in the middle of?

I move back down the hall and go to the science lab. I've got cleaning to do in there anyway, but more than that, I want to figure out what the hell Hicks is up to. Turning the lights on, I approach the terrarium. I rifle through the dirt a little with a small apparatus and find several Tark slugs tucked just beneath.

I shift the dirt back into place and flip the lights. I go back toward the terrarium, only the purple glow remaining, and inspect the critters and their reactions. Their caramel-colored skin has something of an iridescence to it under these lights.

What are you doing in here, Dr. Hicks?

CHAPTER FOURTEEN
CAN'T CATCH A BREAK

I arrive home, my list of struggles growing, my burdens increasing. I'm not much a man of religion or of politics, but I have learned to embrace the transcendental— my back bedroom, a designated quiet place to escape. I have various pages pulled from magazines and books, all taped and sticky-tacked across my ceilings and walls.

Peaceful streams.

Quiet rivers.

Beautiful women.

Cars.

Even a few guitars.

I can't say that I narrow in on anyone in particular when I zone out, but the collage of images puts my mind at ease. I collapse onto the bed that I rarely sleep on, gazing upon them until I put myself into a trance, exploring the inner recesses of my mind. I see so much— big, bold, and breathtaking things, people, and places. It's my dreamworld, my escape, my safe place.

I enjoy my way here when I run from reality. It's a habit I picked up from my mother in her later years. May God bless her. Some kind of experimental therapy by Hicks that kept her sane at least half the time. As for the other half, God only knows. Before I imagine my way off to a distant waterfall or an idyllic beach with beautiful women, there's a pounding at the front door. Peeking out the kitchen window, I notice the Towncar parked outside, its rear window now replaced. I run across to the other side of the house, looking for Dave, but he's nowhere to be seen. Not only that, all the lights are off in his house, uncharacteristic of his normal nocturnal routine. The pounding gets louder. I grab the nine-millimeter he's given me, take the safety off, and peer out the peephole on my front door. I can't rightfully open it and hold the gun at the same time. The man that harassed me before stands just outside with a sawed-off double-barrel shotgun in his right hand.

"I'm sorry. It's not a good time," I call out.

The man's voice booms gruffly, "Mr. Preakle, you know what we're here for. Don't make an example out of yourself. The last thing Cove Ridge needs is *another* bloody mess to clean up on your account. Call the cops and you're dead. You understand?"

"I've got a gun," I declare. "I don't want to get angry."

"Ha! And I, a shotgun, my accomplices in the car are all armed as well. You like that word, armed? Don't you, Preakle? Let me in, and I'll break it down plainly."

What? I've got nothing smart to say. No good comeback, just a loser, a soon to be victim on the evening news. *What the hell? You only live once.*

"Uh... I'm not comfortable with that." I scoff.

What an idiot. If this *is* my final moment on the planet, I die with my tail tucked between my stumpy legs.

"Alright, fine," he says. "Put the briefcase on the porch in the next five minutes with the $9,000, and we'll let you get on with your life. I'd hate to put a slug in that pretty shoulder of yours." The man steps off the porch, gets in the car, and they drive away, certain to come back again in a few minutes.

Slug... there's a double entendre if I ever heard one. This is unexpected. I guess I've called the guy's bluff once more. The threat's intensifying, though. As the vehicle drives away, something on my welcome mat catches my eye. I flick the light on. There's no bluff here. A severed arm sits right in front of me, blood dripping and through the cracks to the ground beneath.

How twisted are these people?

I keep Dave's pistol close, turning the porch light off to minimize suspicion. Going against the harasser's edict, I pick up the phone to call the cops. The line's dead. These guys are a step ahead. I'll give them that. I look out the other window. Joan's lights are off, too. I go outside and cautiously cross to Dave's mobile home, knocking on the door several times. There's blood on the ground next to his usual beer drinking spot. A collage of cans is scattered in a less than impressive pattern. I pound it again, the cheap vinyl door nearly buckling.

"Dave... Dave... are you okay in there?"

There's no reply. I grab the hide-a-key beneath his mat. There's only been one other time in the three years we've been neighbors I've done this, and that was because he'd locked himself out and was too wasted to get himself in the bed. I flick the lights on and go to his telephone, attempting to reach the cops. No dial tone. The clock's ticking, and I've left nothing on my porch to appease the harasser.

"Dave? Are you here? Buddy, I'm trying to get the cops. These guys have cut the phone lines."

I move toward the back of the house, tiptoeing around unfinished pieces of taxidermy, beer cans, and newspapers scattered all over the floor. Dave's second bedroom doubles as his studio for prep work. I flip the light on. No one there, just blood on the floor. Given his line of work, anything's possible, but I fear the worst, considering the bloody arm.

I step out front. Stolz is outside, waiting for me. There's still no sign of Dave.

"What are you doing in there, Preakle? Where's Dave?"

"I was looking for him. It's not like him to be gone this time of night," I reply, my breath elevated, the clock ticking.

He scoffs. "I know that. I live here, too. Still not a clear answer on why you're in this man's house. I guess it's not quite breaking and entering since you had access to a key."

I cool myself down. I know he means well, but that doesn't change my tight timeline.

"Of course not. I have nothing to gain. This guy's worth about fourteen cents, and that's *if* you count the jackrabbit taxidermy. I guess he could sell some of his empties to one of those cash for cans joints."

Stolz shakes his head. "Quite the comedian, aren't you? What was that commotion earlier? I saw the car speed away."

I shake my head. "I'm not really sure. I'm trying to piece it together."

"Piece what together?" he asks.

"Look, you know I'm alright with some chit-chat now and then, but I've got to run. Let me know if you see Dave. I'm a little concerned."

"Alright. Don't panic just yet. I'm sure he just went down to the beer barn."

I nod, thinking of the bloody arm on my porch, my impending doom. I'm down to one minute now.

"By the way, the phones are down."

"Yeah," Stolz replies. "I've heard some complaints. I had one of those bag phones installed in my car recently. The quality's hit and miss, but it's better than nothing. I'll have the phone company out first thing in the morning to investigate."

I approach the house. I'm thankful my porch light's off. Upon further review, there's no sign of the arm, or the blood, either. My garden hose nozzle is positioned in a different spot just above a drying puddle of water. As for the cash, my nicely pressed Andrew Jacksons remain side by side, still untouched. I pull out nine stacks and drop them into the briefcase, and lay them out on the porch. I turn off the lights in the house, the nine-millimeter close by, locked and loaded. The Towncar pulls up. I hear the thug stepping up outside.

"It's all here," he says in the direction of the car. "Let's go."

I breathe a sigh of relief. I guess that's what I'm feeling. Then again, I'm not really sure.

In a matter of days, I've found a dead body, lost my job, and discovered my boss is an uncloseted slug sucker. Meanwhile, I'm sitting on a shortened stack of cash with an unidentified mob roaming my trailer park, and dropping bloody arms on my porch. Not one cop in sight, either. I should be on edge, considering the tension I'm up against, but I'm too exhausted to fight it.

1969

I'm in the hospital room, watching my procedure as it unfolds. Typically, a man doesn't die under sedation, but I'm pretty sure I did. I swear, I see myself there on that operation table while hovering just above. The amputation's short and sweet. The medical staff in the room carry on with their usual banter. It's only a few minutes before the bone saw is out, and they're prepping to drill into my decaying arm. As the doctor reviews the charts and the test results a little closer, their conversation troubles me.

"Are we sure this is the right move?" the taller doctor calls out to the other.

"The government signed off on his chart. Our hands are tied. The disease is in the bone and if we don't operate, it could spread elsewhere. He's lucky it started in the arm and not somewhere more essential."

"The poor bastard's a righty, too. This won't be a fun recovery."

"How many amputations have *you* done?" the shorter doctor asks.

"About four. Never had to on a guy this young or for this reason. We received our orders, though."

"He's gone. Let's get this done. I can't be late for dinner again. The misses will have my hide."

The bone saw starts after the anesthesia's fully set in. It's all a blur after that.

CHAPTER FIFTEEN
BREATHING ROOM

I'm completely gassed from the events of last night, and overcoming the daunting reality that I have more questions than answers. Money's a dirty thing, and it leads people to do dirty things. Prove me wrong.

I get cleaned up and head on to school, a little under the weather—more likely a result of the crazy volley of emotions I've experienced than any sort of sickness. I arrive, punching in at the basement time clock.

I'm already tired of Will Hoblitz. His scratchy voice, his annoying persuasion, and his rude disposition leave me counting down the minutes until his shift ends and I have the school to myself. He's not that bossy, nor particular, just a waste of hot air taking up space to collect a paycheck. I don't think I'll be begging forgiveness for this sentiment anytime soon. I'm sure he sees me much the same.

He looks at me as I arrive. "Greg, it's quitting time for this old man. I've got other stuff to get to. You think you can handle the pool on your own tonight after the kids finish up swimming practice?"

"Yeah, that's not a problem. You've been *more* than gracious with your time," I reply, eyeballing the grump.

"I try my best," he says, rolling his eyes. "I've got to run upstairs to the attic. I forgot something earlier. I'll catch ya tomorrow. You know what to do if you get stuck on something, right?"

"I guess so."

"Good. Don't bother me. It can wait 'til tomorrow," he mutters, sipping on a can of diet soda. He crunches it on the floor beneath his steel-toed boot, and the lingering remnants of the drink splatter across the tiled floor. "Oops, I guess you've got some cleaning up to do, haven't ya?"

"I don't think so, Hoblitz. It can wait 'til tomorrow, right?" I ask, smiling.

"Gonna get smart, are you? Get the gym floors waxed tonight and make sure you air out the basement windows. It gets a little rank down there after practice. I hate coming into the stink the next day when I forget."

I begrudgingly wave at Hoblitz as he goes up the stairs to the attic. In watching him the last couple of days, I've gathered that Fatts is shielding him. I just can't figure out why. Perhaps it's not important. Every damn time I try to mind my business, I end up knee deep in someone else's. The only thing I can come up with is that the guy is hiding something, but he's strange, like many a loner janitor type, so I'm not all that concerned. Who the hell am I to be working up a psychological profile on the old curmudgeon? And though he may be twenty-five years my senior, I know we aren't that different.

***

The day comes to a close, and I end up in Fatts' office. If I'm honest, it's a big cluttered up mess, but he's asked me to leave most of it alone when I come in for evening cleanings. The most interesting thing in the room is a large poster with a pyramid on it, a cup full of neon toned pencils, and an odd assortment of erasers.

His feet are propped up on the desk as he swigs a cup of what I imagine is spiked coffee, the stench of alcohol reeking from his breath. "Yes, sir. I'm doing alright for myself these days, Greggy... You know the worst part of it is, I think I'm slowing down a little. I used to be a 'five nights a week' sort of guy with the misses. We're down to one and neither of us seems to mind. Granted, I've got an entourage of beautiful women to keep me busy around here, but all in all, the supply and demand rules seem to be changing."

I study Fatts' eyes. They're red and worn—bloodshot from sleepless nights.

"Well," I say, "it's only natural for a man's drive to drop, his hairline disappear, and his waistline round things out. Right?"

"Ha-ha. You're a funny guy, Greggy. I knew I liked ya," he says, reaching over and grabbing me by the shoulder.

I pull away. "Well, I've got to get back to the grind," I say, standing up, "and I'm sure you have things to do as well, sir."

There's a tap on the door, and it pops open without warning.

Fatts' face turns flush white as a petite blonde woman enters the room in a pantsuit and overcoat. He drops his feet to the floor, digging around in his desk for a breath mint. I step aside as the woman sits down in the chair across from Fatts.

"I'll be on my way out, sir," I say.

Fatts shakes his head. "Assistant Principal Robbins, what a... pleasant surprise. I'd like... you... to meet Greg Preakle —The Pool Man... our custodian. Greg, Mrs. Robbins is our new assistant principal."

Her face remains stone sour as she extends her hand to shake mine. Her first impression of me is likely not a good one— I missed my morning shower and neglected to shave, so I'm not much better off than my drunken superior.

"Nice to meet you, Mr. Preakle," she says. "Why Pool Man?"

"The pleasure's all mine. I've been cleaning pools for twenty years. It's just a nickname," I reply. Hoblitz's sarcastic voice races through my mind, knowing what a "kiss ass" I really am in these situations.

"Mr. Preakle, you're dismissed," she says, studying me a little closer with her blue eyes as her gaze gravitates toward my nub. "Mr. Fatts, I'd like a word with you privately."

"I hope it's not a four-letter word," Fatts says— his crooked smile and voice tempo showing a growing uncertainty.

I walk out of the room, almost knocking the receptionist, Mindy, over. She has a red cup pressed against the door to eavesdrop.

"Come here, Mr. Preakle. You can listen, too," her tiny voice calls out.

I lean in toward her. Her perfume's strong. The red blouse on her busty frame, a definite temptation to more than just Fatts. As our eyes lock, her warm feelings for the heavyset principal are barely masked.

Robbins' voice grows louder and more commanding. We probably don't even need the cup to hear it. "The place is sloppy. The building's looking like it's gone to hell and back. Our teachers are leaving us for Barton Hills. What's going on around here? The superintendent told me my work was cut out for me, but this is more than I could have expected."

"Well, I guess that's why we have you here now," Fatts says. "I could use the help."

"This isn't something to brush off," Robbins says. "My point is... you're hiring guys... like Greg, you're drunk on the job, and failing to discipline staff the way you should. Not to mention showing favoritism to the ones you shouldn't. I've already dismissed a teacher on your behalf for gross misconduct with a staff member. I'm not here to be a snitch, or to take your job. I'm just here to give you a little gut check, so to speak."

"Don't undermine me so loudly again," Fatts says, a pounding sound coming from behind the door. "This is *my* school, and I'll run it *my* way."

"I've only been here a few hours, John, and I'm finding trouble around every corner."

"I have my way of handling things," he says, his voice unrelenting. "They're just... unorthodox. We've been having a rough go around here."

"From what I've heard, they've cut you slack for years," she says. "I intend to uncover every rock and clean up where I see trouble, John."

"Dismissed!" he yells, a stomping sound bouncing across the room's tile.

Footsteps approach the door. Mindy and I bolt across the room. I pretend to dust the shelves.

"Mr. Preakle, right?" Robbins calls out.

"Yes, ma'am?"

"If you're a true asset to West Riverton ISD and you care about that man in there, do me a favor and straighten him out. Apparently, it's too much to ask of his wife. God bless her."

"I'll do what I can."

"Good talk!" she says, storming out of the room.

I debate about going back in to check on Fatts, eventually opting to do so. I knock briefly and enter the room. Fatts pours more whiskey into his coffee.

He looks up at me. "Preakle, it is what it is. I've been on the bubble for a while now. This new AP coming in, Mrs. Robbins, she's gunning for my job and will have it in no time. Probably 'mopping the floor' with the superintendent, too."

I shake my head. "I doubt it, sir. Give her a shot."

Fatts wipes a little dribble of drool from his lip. "Yeah... I'm just going to take a nap and sleep it off. That always makes it better. I get enough beatings from my old lady as it is."

"Hang in there, Mr. Fatts," I say, patting him on the back.

Fatts nods, his sullen face showing after the heated discussion. "We'll see. Take care, Preakle. Do me a favor and flip that light switch on your way out, please?"

"Not a problem, sir."

For some unknown reason, I hope the bastard straightens himself out before it costs his job.

CHAPTER SIXTEEN
NEIGHBORLY WAY

I make it home. Dave's lights are on. I decide to stop by and check in. He's sitting outside with a Flitz in a large gray sweatshirt. I'm no mother hen, but at a minimum, I've got to do that. It's the neighborly way.

"Evening, Greg."

"Hey. It's good to see you home. I was wondering where you were last night."

"Home is where the heart is," he says, sipping on his evening brew.

I nod.

Dave hands me a beer. "Why are you looking at me like you've seen a ghost?"

"Last night, man, where were you? I saw blood on the porch. I got concerned."

"Oh, that? A client dropped off a boar that wasn't drained properly. I didn't get things washed off before I had to run. I had a meeting to attend," he says.

"Oh? I didn't know you were networked that way, man. Good for you."

Dave scoffs. "I'm a businessman, Greg. I've got to do what I can to get by. Since when do *you* care so much?"

I sigh. "It happened again. The jerk-offs came by, guns loaded and begging for cash. I was wishing I had your six-shooter an arm's length away," I say.

"No shit? I'm sorry, neighbor. I gave you my nine-millimeter. Hopefully, it made a difference this time," he says, crunching his latest beer, and cracking open another.

"I paid 'em. Hopefully, that's the end of this crap. I'm pissed, but I'm useless," I mutter, finishing my drink and pitching it into his quickly growing pile. "You got another one of those?"

"For you, neighbor? Of course."

"Hey listen, man. I'm just racking my brain here. I don't know what the hell I'm mixed up in. This school gig's getting me by, but it seems like I'm just attracting more trouble after starting."

"We talked about this, remember? The goddess of chance? Fate comes full circle, guy. Stop fretting about it and move on. I've got your back. We've just got to get you ready to pull that trigger if those chumps decide to come back around. I guarantee you, once the hammer drops, their asses will split like grass."

"You mean 'their ass *is* grass,' right?"

He sips his beer. "Yeah, sure. Yeah, that's what I meant."

I laugh. Dave certainly has a way of getting me to unload and relax. We need more guys like him around.

"What was your meeting about?"

He sucks air through his teeth. "About?"

"Yeah?"

"It's a business I'm investing in, something up and coming. I can't really say much more just yet, though. I signed a non-disclosure agreement."

Damn. I took it too far. I shouldn't have pried. This stuff has a way of making its way in the open in due time.

"I got it. I'm sorry I overstepped."

"I'll cut you in on the scoop when I can. Just watch yourself, man. These money-grubbing chumps can be relentless— loose cannons blow gigantic holes, you know?"

A wave of fatigue hits me. "I've got to get to bed."

"Keep that gun under your pillow just in case," he says. "I'll keep my eyes peeled, too. That's what neighbors are for. We look out for each other. By the way, I left you some cold ones in the fridge."

"Oh? Thanks for that," I say. "Wait, I'm the one that owes you."

"Buddy, you've done a lot for me the last couple of years. If nothing else, shooting the shit with you beats the hell out of talking to the sky or to Joan. God bless you, man. It's the least I could do," he says, his Cheshire grin putting me further at ease.

to judge, or we define "good for" me the best couple of years. It's all in our hands, so we act every moment, the breath of eternity, the sky so far to follow. And here you can see, the Lord's good do." He says, "the Christian's great purpose, our intelligence.

CHAPTER SEVENTEEN
WHERE'S HOBLITZ?

I arrive at work at high noon. There's no sign of Hoblitz. I explore the campus, carrying on with my duties. The garbage bins are filling quickly, the bathrooms need cleaning, and the windows are well overdue for a washing. It only takes a couple of hours for this place to lose order. I walk toward the administration office.

I'm not indebted to the old man, but at a minimum, I owe it to him to make sure he didn't just keel over somewhere.

I approach Fatts' office, breezing right past Mindy, who seems more concerned with painting her fingernails than greeting me.

I knock once and let myself in.

"Hey, good afternoon," I say. Fatts isn't alone. AP Robbins sits right next to him, reviewing the district's policy and procedure manual. The look in his eyes tells me things at the school will change drastically if he wants to keep his job. I don't really feel sorry for him. I'm actually appreciative of Robbins' efforts. As long as she leaves me alone, I don't really care.

"Greg, come in. You've met AP Robbins already."

"Hello," she says, reaching out her hand to shake mine.

"Hi. Nice to see you."

"What's on your mind, Mr. Preakle?" Fatts says, one hundred percent more diplomatic and sober than the last time we spoke. "How can we help you? AP Robbins and I are just strategizing ways to streamline things around here. To give the school a good 'kick in the pants,' so to speak.

I nod. "Well, I was looking for Mr. Hoblitz. Have you seen him around this morning? Did he call in sick?"

"Come to think of it, I haven't," he says.

I peer around Fatts' office and note the clutter, further realizing what a slob the guy is — or, perhaps, has always been. Surely, AP Robbins isn't falling for the smoke the man's blowing.

"AP Robbins, can I have a word with Mr. Preakle, privately? I'll come into your office in a few minutes."

Her plastic reaction seems staged. "Sure, we can pick this up later."

As she exits the room, Fatts waves me over closer, mumbling with his teeth gritted together, "Why don't you go check the attic? He loiters around up there sometimes. Don't make a scene, though. I got AP Robbins doing a damn colonoscopy on this place right now."

"Okay, I'll do that," I say, nodding toward a filing cabinet across the room. "You might want to clean up a little better..." I point to a pair of white laced underwear hanging from a drawer.

Becoming fidgety, Fatts moves over to move the items out of sight. "Thanks, Preakle. Hopefully Robbins' eyes were more focused on that manual than my... impulse control issues."

I approach the mini blinds on Fatts' west window, raking a cloud of dust off.

"If you find Hoblitz, go easy on him. She's already torn into him. He's an asset I'm not ready to lose yet."

"An asset? You told me he was a real piece of work before I started. Why the change of heart?"

"There's no change," he says. "He may not be my favorite human being on the planet, but that doesn't mean I hate the man."

"Alright, then."

Fatts scoffs, shaking his head. "You expecting me to fire him already, or what?"

"No. I just see lots of potential for opportunity around here."

"Of course you do, Preakle. It's a new job. Once you get a little more mileage, your philosophy will change."

I resent the sentiment, my simple reply the best passive jab. "I'll check the attic."

"Keep me posted. And play it smart with AP Robbins. She's watching you, too."

"I will," I say, excusing myself.

***

Class is in session again after lunch hour, and I head toward the attic. Rifling my way through keys, I unlock the door. The stench of the dead raccoon has dissipated considerably from my last trip up. On the far west side of the floor, I notice the locked door Hoblitz told me to ignore before. After a few attempts, I conclude the keys I've been supplied will not let me in. A purple hue shines beneath the crack at the bottom. Noises coming from beneath mimic that of a television or a radio. I tap on the door. There's no answer.

I'm seriously wondering what's going on at this point. I've been witness to sketchy lives, but for some reason, I thought school was exempt much the same as clergy. I guess not.

"Mr. Hoblitz, are you in there, sir?" I call out. I knock again. "Hello, Mr. Hoblitz?" There's no reply. There's an attic phone on the wall next to the door, so I call down to administration and get Mindy.

"Hey, Mindy. It's Greg Preakle. Can you see if Mr. Fatts is available?"

"Sure, one moment."

I knock on the door again while I wait for Fatts to come on the phone. "Mr. Hoblitz, are you in there, sir? None of my keys are working."

"Hey, Mr. Preakle," Mindy says. "Here's John."

"Thanks."

"Preakle, what's the deal?" Fatts says. "Everything okay? I can't even recall the last time I had a call from the attic phone."

"John, I still can't find Hoblitz. I've checked all over campus. There's a room up here I can't get into, though. I've tried knocking and can hear something on in the background. Do you have a key?"

"Yeah," he says with a sigh. The sound of crinkling mini blinds comes through, leading me to pull the phone away from my ear. "His truck's outside," Fatts continues, "so he must be around somewhere. I'll meet you up there. Give me a couple of minutes."

"Let's meet halfway." I come back down the steps and make eye contact with Fatts in the middle of the long school corridor near the students' lockers. Dr. Hicks exits the school infirmary, interrupting us unexpectedly.

"Hey, guys. I'm sorry to butt in. I just need to speak with Mr. Fatts a moment in private."

The look in Fatts' eyes tells me he's uncomfortable with the arrangement. "Sure, let's go in here," he replies, his teeth gritted.

I walk over to the lockers nearest the office, wiping dust from them, hoping my ears may pick up on some of the communication on the other side of the wall.

Hicks' voice is low and soft enough that I can't quite follow.

"That's just going to have to work. I know we need more participation, but this will just have to do," Fatts says. "We'll discuss more about this at our next presentation."

I keep busy, moving across the hallway to the lockers on the opposite side as Fatts comes out a little flustered. He directs our conversation back to Hoblitz. "So, no sign of the old man, huh?" he asks, lifting his pants a notch back above his waist. I think he's dropped a pant size since we first met. I don't say anything, though.

"Nope. Hopefully, he's just camped out in there. Have you had issues like this with him in the past?"

"Only the last couple of years, since he... picked up a new habit."

"New habit? At his age? I hope it's just Geritol."

"I don't challenge him, Preakle. He takes care of things... he takes care of me."

As we go back up the stairs, Fatts reaches into his pocket, cycling through a substantial keyring. "Yeah, this is the one." He hands it to me. "You can hang onto it. Just between us, this is another break room for a select few."

"Is that right?" I ask, less than candid, trusting my growing rapport with the man. "And who might that be? Ladies you swoon over?"

"No, no. Nothing like that, Preakle. I may be a man of indiscretions, but I'm smart enough to watch myself more closely on the school grounds, at least outside my office, anyhow."

I unlock the padlock, pulling it away from the door. Fatts flips the lights on as we enter, and a foul odor hits. A countless stock of vending machine snacks line the walls. Roaches crawl all over the floors, their droppings everywhere.

Videocassettes with lewd names are strewn about. The small wood paneled television in the room's corner is still on— its snowy screen statically crowing at us. Hoblitz is crashed out on the couch with a pile of beer cans crunched all around him. Before I have time to react, the VCR's auto-rewind feature starts the tape over again. A ridiculous and familiar song comes on, synthesizers in full swing, the crazy letters and editing job, amateur at best.

"*Play one... play all... play one... play all... Castle Productions Presents— Twisted Hacks... cable TV's bloodiest quiz show!*"

The host comes on the screen.

"Oh, yes, Preakle... you'll appreciate this," Fatts says, resting his hand on my shoulder.

I scoff as we make eye contact. "I hate it!"

Fatts shakes his head and grins. "So touchy. And why is that? A little trash TV can do a weary man some good now and then. It breaks up the monotony. Gets you away from the mundane." He takes a seat on the far end of the couch, seemingly unphased by the room's poor upkeep, and later opening a confiscated Twinkie and heaving its contents into his mouth. "Take a load off, Preakle. No one will miss us."

"What about Robbins?" I ask.

"Pfft. I gave her a list of busy work to keep her all over campus. The attic's not on the agenda, Preakle. Relax."

I'm bothered by Fatts, but coming to accept his quirks. Everyone's had a weird boss at some point in their life, right? The degree to their weirdness is certainly subjective to the audience. There's an unspoken relativity to it all, I suppose. This guy's kept this job longer than he should have. He just knows how to say the right things at just the right times to smooth things over. No convictions with lying when it works to his benefit, either.

Hoblitz wakes and sits up, clearly a little startled. "Well, shit from the sky and burn me red! What are you doing in here?"

I look at Fatts, dropping my eyebrows, pulling my head away.

"You're late for work!" Fatts says. "And we've got the new AP on campus! She was already on you yesterday," he says gruffly. "I should be asking you. What aren't you doing?!"

Hoblitz waves him off, still inebriated. "Ah! Go suck a slug."

I expect a reaction out of Fatts, but there's less. He's like a useless parent in a bad dream, his focus drifting to the television. The question cues on the screen as music intensifies, and the blue helmet contestant spins the wheel.

My eyes gravitate toward the far corner of the room. I've completely missed the purple glow I'd seen from under the door until now. There's a terrarium in here, too.

Standing up to approach it, Hoblitz's gravelly chirp fills the room. "Stay back. Those aren't yours!" he says. "You know how hard I have to work for those?"

Peering into the dirt tank, a number of little critters move around frantically— the container's full of Tark slugs. There's a bottle to the side of it marked, "High-pH pool water."

"Getting cracked out on these things at work, Mr. Hoblitz?" I ask, looking at Principal Fatts.

"Nope," he says. "Not on the clock, anyway."

Fatts nods. "Good. Keep it that way. We need to re-home these guys to the science lab before AP Robbins spots them. They'll blend in better there."

Hoblitz stands up and stretches. "Yeah, fine. Well, I better get back to work."

As he exits the room, Fatts follows close behind. "You better!" he calls out. "And Preakle, keep your mouth shut about this. I didn't plan on you... seeing this so soon."

I shake my head. "I don't know what to say. You guys are overexposing slugs with the school's pool water, too?"

"We will now and then at the end of a long week," Fatts says as he waves me and Hoblitz out of the room. "Go ahead and lock her up. The trouble with getting too many of 'em too close with overexposure is they get a hyper cluster going."

"Hyper cluster?" I ask, latching the door shut. "What do you mean?"

"They group together. They'll take over a room if they're unsupervised too long."

"Oh, really? Has it happened before?"

"Twice. Hoblitz keeps them confined in the attic mostly, though. We'll let a raccoon loose now and then to clean house when it gets out of hand. As to keeping them confined, a towel under the doorjamb usually gets the job done."

"How resourceful," I say, chuckling. Such brilliant minds I'm working with here.

Fatts nods. "We're going to have to move this bachelor's shithole elsewhere. AP Robbins already has a goldmine of reasons to run me out of here."

"I can see that," I reply. "We don't need kids sucking slugs here on campus."

Fatts agrees. "What a PTA meeting that would be... not to mention the superintendent's colorful reaction."

Hoblitz and I go toward the basement while Fatts heads down toward the administration wing of the school.

"It wasn't much of a shift today," Hoblitz says, "but what he doesn't know won't hurt him."

"Sheesh, don't you ever work?" I ask.

CHAPTER EIGHTEEN
NEW OUTLOOK

I enter the pool area, making eye contact with Hoblitz. He's busy skimming the water. It's indoors, so there's little to do.

"Hey, I thought you were already off the clock today."

"The pool was in disarray, Greg. Someone's got to pull their weight around here! And I needed to make up for some lost hours the other day, anyway."

"You got caught slacking off?" I chide. "And I suppose *you* had nothing to do with the dead slugs I found in the pool earlier?"

He shakes his head. "Nope! I never mix business with pleasure. Not my style. It's too risky."

"What's stopping Robbins from finding your attic hideaway? She'll be chirping to the superintendent in a heartbeat when she catches wind of this."

"I'm not the enabler," Hoblitz says. "Fatts is. I doubt she'll bother, though. We'll just tell her the attic has vermin problems. That ought to work," he replies.

"I'm going to wax the floors in the hallway and lunchroom if you need me for anything," I say.

"Alright, Greg. If we don't cross paths again today, can you come in early tomorrow? I have some other stuff to do in the morning that would be good for you to learn. I've got to get myself retired one of these days. This lady's gonna work me into an early grave if I'm not careful. Meet me at 0900 in the basement."

"Sure. I'll meet you then."

***

I arrive at nine the next morning as discussed and the school day's in full swing. Slipping in the side door, I approach the time clock and punch my card. A rustling sound emerges on the opposite side of the basement. I move toward it. Something envelops my throat. I can't swallow. Death's in the air again.

I don't know what the deal is. I just know it. With all the crap going on around here, it was bound to happen at some point.

Call it intuition.

Call it fate.

Call me screwed.

A trickle of blood streams from the water heater closet.

I pinch my nose. The odor is unbearable—like stale, dead fish piled up in a landfill and sitting in the sun a week too long. As I pull the door open, what's left of the late William Hoblitz collapses to the floor covered in electrical burns — more a crispy critter than a pliable human.

Damn. I can't take any more of this. I didn't sign up to keep finding dead bodies. I sure as hell didn't kill him. I'm not that kind of psycho. I'm not the unreliable narrator you hate. I swear. Just a normal guy trying to get by.

The char marks on the edges of the water heater and its electrical connection leave me convinced Hoblitz is a victim of unfortunate circumstances, his body the grounding point for a gas influenced explosion. A poor old man dead and gone just weeks from retirement. Reaching behind the tank, I shut off the gas line and unplug the heater as my heart pounds through my neck. The walls of the school close in around me as panic overtakes. I'm seconds away from fainting if I don't sit down and find water.

I head upstairs, bolting towards the administration offices. I skip Mindy, tap on Mr. Fatts' door and plow right in. I've clearly startled him as he rushes to put a flask of Old Tymer's whiskey back into the drawer.

"Sheesh, Preakle? Can't you knock? What are you doing here so early, anyway?" he asks, his teeth gritted.

"John, it's Hoblitz. He's..."

Fatts interrupts, the light reflecting on him brightly. "What?"

"Will Hoblitz is dead."

"No. No, he's not," Fatts says, sinking into his chair, running his fingers across the top of his bald head.

"Afraid so."

"You've got to be joking. I just talked to him a few hours ago when he was opening the school. The old man had the audacity to swear at me in front of the other teachers. He's really... dead?"

I nod.

"Great god of Minerva!" he replies, jumping up from his desk.

"Goddess of Minerva..." I interject.

"Smart ass," Fatts says, his well-endowed gut continuing to shrink with the passing days. "The superintendent will nail my ass to the wall."

"John, I'm concerned... I don't think he died of natural causes..."

"How'd he die, Preakle?" he asks, his breath escalating and his face reddening as we approach the door to his office.

"How should I know? Just follow me into the basement. It looks like some kind of water heater explosion or a gas leak."

I struggle to catch my breath. My stomach's in knots. I've just been given a lifetime supply of queasiness. How's that for karma? I'll take Wonka's chocolate any day.

"Damn it," he says. "Have you told anyone else, Greg?"

"No, sir," I say, my chest palpitating out of sync with the rest of me.

"Try to play it calm and we'll figure this out. I don't want the entire school up in arms. The old man was already a ticking time bomb."

Walking through the administration offices, Fatts makes eyes at Mindy, the kind that require no words to send a message of affection. I can tell from the look on her face, she knows something's wrong, but at least has the decency not to ask right now. We head out of the outer office, gliding through the halls and toward the basement. Fatts and I approach the water heater closet.

"Man alive. He *is* crispy. Poor bastard." Fatts says. "Nature. It strikes when we least expect it. Right?"

"I guess..." I reply. "Do we need to call the cops?"

Fatts shakes his head. "Well, Preakle, I know you want to be a good Samaritan and turn this into the authorities, but with AP Robbins up my ass and the superintendent close behind, I can't afford this on my watch. Besides, cops on this kind of scene won't do us any good. He's already dead. It just looks like one of those freak things. Before we go out and declare this a damn crime scene, let's assume the best. As far as we know, it's just an accident, right? They'll load the galoot on a gurney, throw a little makeup on him, and we'll see him down at Cedar City under the hot lights at the wake in a day or two. Hopefully, you've learned the ropes well enough to... to get by."

I'm perplexed by his demeanor. "Mr. Fatts, I think we ought to call the police. More trouble could be abrew. Hoblitz was not a likeable fellow, nor was he inept with this kind of stuff. This could have been tampered with."

Fatts grabs at his belt loop and tugs. "Yeah. I'll uh... I'll handle the 911 call. You keep the area sealed off. We'll get someone down here soon."

"Good," I say, running my tongue beneath my lower lip. It's a strange habit, a nervous tic really. "I cut off the gas and pulled the plug earlier in case of further mechanical failure."

"Good thinking, Preakle. Let's see if we can get this guy out of here without disrupting the school day. Hopefully, they can wheel him out the side door."

"Okay. Yeah, that would be better, wouldn't it?" I say.

"Keep the area roped off. I don't want anyone to hit the showers after PE class or smell this guy. We'll just tell them there's plumbing issues, and they'll have to wait until they get home to rinse off."

CHAPTER NINETEEN
BLURRING REALITY

I'm back home.

Hoblitz is still dead. Blown to smithereens like that guy on *Platoon,* only this time it's a school basement.

The closest thing I have to go on at this point is knowing that the old timer was sucking slugs with Fatts, and they had a break room to escape to. There's probably some kind of off-the-record community of slug suckers, and it's happening near the school. Yeah. I bet that's it, but why's he dead? What's the motive? There are lots of explanations to consider.

Of course, there's the thought he got a little off center after a slug suck, took an unpleasant trip, and screwed himself over.

Or maybe the pipe supplying the gas got perforated, a mere side effect of its age, and he was the lucky victim.

That could have been me. Shit.

Or, perhaps the old man had a heart attack while he was working near the water heater, dropped his pipe in the wrong spot and sparks flew. Yikes.

Another idea, he and Fatts had a business deal go sideways, and he disposed of him, making it look like an accidental death, ripped straight from a goofy ending on *Murder, She Wrote.*

I don't want Fatts to be the killer, though. Of course, he's involved. Hell, he could even be the one driving the damn car off the cliff, and here I am, still packed in the trunk and along for the ride. How stupid would that be? It's like a terrible movie ending I've seen a million times over. The entire thing builds up. You get to the final scene and realize the killer's exactly the guy that you thought it was the whole time. That makes for a crap ending, doesn't it?

Real life murder cases work that way, though. It's a brother-in-law. An ex-spouse. A neighbor. A co-worker. An unhinged boss. Another philanderer. And I guess that's what this is. A real-life murder case. I'm hurting for the guy. When someone says "life should end with a bang," I don't imagine that's quite what they meant.

I know this much. Something went sideways, and I guess we're back to square one again.

I can't give Fatts my best anymore. I'm not going to draw any lines in the sand and make an enemy, though. Certainly, no plans for a confrontation just yet. I'm just making an intentional effort to watch my back. There was no disclaimer that came with this job, no warning label. Just a friendly face and a lot of beer in a fishing boat. What's a man to do? Find another job, stat. I don't have enough bucks to just quit, though. The Towncar goons pretty well cleaned me out.

As for the agenda tonight, it won't be light.

Heavy.

Yeah. Definitely heavy.

A little boob tube, processed meats and cheese cubes, a couple of cold ones, and I'm ready to doze.

Yeah. Right as rain.

1987

I let myself in through mom's front door, the stench of death awakening my darkest demons.

"Mom... oh, dear God! Mom!"

She's on the floor, her orange pill bottle across her chest, a few little pink pills strewn about. There's no note. No closure— she's just gone. I study her. Her pale, cold face... breathless, lifeless, and dead for days. I head to the kitchen telephone and call 911, struggling to find the words as I give the name, address, and reason for my call. I drop to the floor.

Losing her this way just feels wrong—how she could fathom ending it all, and at mine and dad's expense. What a selfish waste— spoiling and rotting away, decayed and gone. No goodbyes.

I'm in tears as the ambulance arrives. This hurts differently than Denny—so differently.

CHAPTER TWENTY
CLEAN UP

1991

I start my shift in the teacher's lounge, tidying up around the refrigerators and vending machines. There's the usual chatter and banter between staff members. I mostly tune it out or put on a cassette with a set of headphones. It gets sweaty under there quickly, though, so it's rarely a long-winded affair.

I hear the clomp of AP Robbins shoes coming down the hall. The voices in the room fall silent. I don't know what I think about her. I'm kind of old school. I've never responded well to female authority. It's probably something generational, the way my pop raised me. She's good looking, though. It's a bit of a conundrum because there's some part of me within that wants to please her.

Robbins stands only five feet tall, but her distinct, high-pitched voice can still rattle the ceiling tiles. I can't make out what she's saying to some of the other teachers across the room, but their body language tells me all I need to know. She's in charge, and they're not.

She leaves the room; her black clad business attire, further testament to her commitment to a higher calling. The energy in the room's weaker after she's left, a little more cautious than before, too. They're probably all gossiping about her, making stupid little inside jokes about her quirks, and hoping they don't get caught. It's cliquey around here. That's just how these kinds of employment situations go. All I can say is, it's not for me. The lone wolf approach is underrated. I don't want to get stuck in the middle of it all, so I just hover about. It's smarter, easier, and a hell of a lot less baggage. I've got too much to do, anyhow— way too much.

I walk out of the lounge and go down the hall. Coach Simmons pops out of the gymnasium door. "Mr. Preakle, we've got vomit on the ball court. Can you take care of it?"

I want to ignore him, but I need to stay off AP Robbins' radar. It's too early to get choosy. "Yeah. No problem, Coach. Just a minute."

As I come into the gym, Simmons shows little concern for the boys. "Yep. The baked bean casserole isn't agreeing with 'em, I'm afraid."

"I thought it looked a little soupy today," I reply. "Oh, what a joy... just another day in the life of a janitor at West Riverton High."

Simmons grins at me like he's thrilled to see me work, to watch my hips swivel. The mop going back and forth across the waxed floor. Weirdo. Like I've mentioned, he's quite the character, maybe a bit the jerk, but mostly bumpkin. We enter the gym, and I get the squeegee out of the storeroom on the west end. All the players, shooting airball after airball— a room full of losers.

"Good grief, coach." I mutter as I wipe up the mess. "Don't we have any talent left around here?"

"Afraid not. There's another mediocre year in store for the Spartans. I'm concerned this new AP is going to shut down the athletics program altogether."

"I don't think she can do that... And replace it with what?" I ask.

"Who knows?" he mutters. "A bunch of robots and computers, I reckon."

"Well, computers are the future."

"I get that, but sports are an escape. It gives these kids purpose."

"Purpose? It's just high school sports, man. They're not that big a deal," I tease.

He smiles at me, half embarrassed. "We were teammates, Greg. You don't ever think back to those days and feel thankful for the opportunity?"

"Not really," I say, shaking my head.

"Whatever. I'm talking about teamwork and camaraderie. Skill building. All those essential things you'll take with you everywhere you go. Truth is, Greg, I'm sweating my butt off to keep this job and if Jenny catches wind that I'm due for a layoff, she'll flip a lid and divorce me."

"Well, I mean, there are other schools, right? What's the big deal about making a change? You know, moving the Simmons family out of Riverton?"

It's a selfish question. Maybe I'm greasing the wheels a little to get this guy out of my hair. I don't know.

He blows his whistle, motioning to the boys to run some laps around the gym. "It just doesn't feel right. I moved away when I went to college and this sleepy old town kept beckoning me home. It's where I belong."

"Alright, alright. Don't get sappy about Riverton. We both know it's just an old town full of trouble." I move toward the door. "Later, Coach."

"Thanks, Greg."

I walk out of the gym, prepping to review what's left on my checklist for the day. I owe it to the school to admit that working here isn't all bad in spite of character flaws in administration and an untimely demise. That could have happened anywhere. Yeah, it really could have. So, if I just go with that frame of thinking, it helps me rationalize and decompress some of the tension. As for the work, the physical nature of the job keeps me young and gives me purpose. Perhaps I'm just more empowered with Hoblitz gone. I don't know. Or it's that extra umph recognizing AP Robbins' attention to the minutia is more accountability. Some of us need that whether we admit it or not. On the surface, we hate it, but in all reality, it's exactly what we need.

As for my current work area, it's a work in progress, and I'm still making adjustments. There's not much down here beyond the generators, various plumbing accesses, the custodian supply rooms and workspaces, and the showers. Just above my old, recycled desk, I've added a set of Motley Crue and Guns N' Roses posters to keep me company. It's one of the few areas in life I rebel, just a little. I love loud rock and roll, especially stuff from the Sunset Strip. And after hours, I can't help myself from blasting it through the school's intercom system.

I fill out my stack of checklists and tasks, prepping to move on to my favorite duty of the day— the pool. The clomp of AP Robbins's shoes grows louder as she comes down the steps toward the less than tidy basement work area. Isn't it ironic how the guy in charge of cleaning the school keeps every room in the building clean but his own? I debate on if I should make a beeline somewhere else or just face whatever ugly music AP Robbins may bring. I don't think I've done anything to upset or offend her yet. I stand up and grab the broom to make myself look busier, swooping a pile of mice droppings beneath the neighboring storage cabinets and just out of sight.

"Uh... ma'am," I call out, quickly making eye contact. "I'm sorry. I wasn't expecting anyone down here this afternoon."

She responds curtly, resting her hand on her hip as she checks her clipboard and runs her finger down a list. "And I know we met already, but I just don't do well with names the first few times. There you are, Gregory Preakle, the school custodian?"

"Yes, ma'am."

"Very good," she says, making a mark on her list. "You don't have a problem with me checking in on you, do you?"

I sigh. "Na."

She moves toward my desk, tearing down my posters.

"Hey!" I yell. "I just bought those."

I'm brave enough to say something. Or dumb enough, I don't know.

She shakes her head. "Such an outstanding example. Look at these guys. A bunch of grown men with more hair and promiscuity than I know how to stand! I'm a little disgusted with your professionalism, Mr. Preakle. If the kids saw a role model like you listening to this junk, they'd follow suit, and we can't be having that," she says, crumpling the posters and throwing them in the garbage. "Look at this dump! There's dust everywhere. What have you been doing with your time? The windows need cleaning. The trees need tidying. The grass needs cutting. We need a proper groundskeeper."

"Ma'am, with all due respect, Mr. Hoblitz was handling a lot of this, too, before his, uh, his early retirement."

She scoffs. "Don't pawn your weaknesses off on someone else. I don't play nice, and I don't play favorites! I've done my rounds and all I see around here is a bunch of garbage and things left unfinished, rotting, and molding. I don't know what exactly you think you're responsible for around here, but no matter what it is, it seems to me your work efforts are inferior. We've got head lice, flu outbreaks, and regular reports of maggots in the garbage bins. I've even heard of dead slugs in the swimming pool baskets. You better explain yourself before I send you packing and replace you. Just step up your game a little around here, please? With Mr. Hoblitz gone, someone's got to pick up the slack. Can you do that for me?"

I nod, keeping a straight face.

"Come to my office, Mr. Preakle. I've been working on a new list of duties for you," she says.

As we go up the stairs and out of the basement, the unruly assistant principal gets distracted by a pair of students making out in the hallway and paces away toward them. She turns around. "We'll touch base later. I need to tend to this. I *will* have order and discipline in this institution!"

I'm startled by a crashing sound in the basement.

"What's going on? Who's down there?" I call out.

Making my way down, I notice one of the shelving units at the back of the room has crashed to the floor along with a bunch of nails and tools spread in multiple directions. Before I can get across to it, there's a loud squeaking noise and a click. The room's never been well lit in the far corner. I shine my flashlight toward it and notice a door behind where the shelving unit once stood. I approach it carefully, shining the light across the room to ensure I'm alone. Moving toward the door, I work to unlatch its aged hinges.

AP Robbins's heels clomp back into earshot as she descends the steps. There's a growing calmness in her voice, less tense than our previous encounter. "Excuse me, Mr. Preakle. I heard a commotion down here and just wanted to make sure you were okay."

"Yes, um... thank you. Something knocked one of our shelves over. I'll just be tidying it up and finding new homes for some of this stuff."

"Good grief. I'm glad you weren't hurt. I'm not here to micromanage your day. I just wanted to be sure you're okay."

"All's well," I reply. "Thanks for checking in."

"Good. Well, I assume you'll get this area cleaned up, then. It's a rat's nest!"

"Yes, ma'am."

Shortly after the brief discussion, she exits the stairwell. I pull out and uncrumple my posters, mounting them back on the wall. I'm unable to jar the door on the far side of the room loose and I don't want to bring unnecessary attention to it during school hours, so I'll wait until the time's right. Something about it seems intentionally masked and hidden away.

CHAPTER TWENTY-ONE
LONE RANGER

With no replacement for Hoblitz in sight, it seems the unspoken expectation for me is to keep up with all duties on my own. AP Robbins's close watching eyes are also right on me, so the pressure's on to do a better job. I've re-homed myself to the old man's former workspace. His workbench and tools are still there. The fellow certainly made sure his stool was more comfortable than the shoddy one he let me have. I move a few of the personal items from my work area and drop it on the desk. Rifling through one of Hoblitz's drawers, I find a stack of cash. Its bills organized from smallest to largest, amounting to about a thousand bucks. There's a tacked sticky note on top that has the eve of Hoblitz's death written on it. It's marked in the same handwriting as mine was.

"Your last payday," I mumble.

I consider why he's paid in cash and assume Fatts must be cutting corners in every way possible with the payment methods used on personnel. I approach the door revealed by the collapsed shelving unit, again working to pry it open. It just doesn't seem to budge.

Walking over to administration, I intend to speak with Fatts about my discovery, and to turn in the money from Hoblitz's workstation. Mindy's not at her desk, so I knock on the door, prepping to let myself in.

"Mr. Fatts? Can I have a word with you, sir?"

"In a minute, Preakle," he says from behind the door. "I'm a little... preoccupied."

"I'll take a seat."

"Give me five minutes. Go make a cup of coffee or something," he calls out.

A few minutes later, Mindy exits the office, her hair in disarray, her blouse buttoned in the wrong places.

"Mr. Preakle, Mr. Fatts will see you now. I apologize for the delay," she says, the breathiness in her voice more pronounced.

I nod my head as I go into the office. Fatts' breath remains elevated as he waves me in.

"Gregory Preakle, to what do I owe *this* pleasure?"

"Sir, I've got a couple of things. First, I promoted myself to Hoblitz's work area and stumbled across this," I say, handing him the stack of cash.

"Oh, wow. Aren't you a good Samaritan, Preakle?"

"I do what I can."

He nods and smiles. "And second?"

"Second, one of the shelving units collapsed earlier. Ever since the incident with Hoblitz, it seems like someone's been poking around in the basement. Did you know about the door behind the shelves?"

"Oh, yeah... it's been a millennium since that's been used, though. There's a tornado shelter in there that we used to take the kids into. It's connected to the old subway tunnel."

"Yeah? It runs across town, then?" I ask.

"You bet," he says. "I haven't walked that route down there in ages, though. It's like a hobo's haven. I'm not interested in hob-knobbing with the likes of their kind if I don't have to."

"Is there any reason someone would have tried to plow into the school from the tunnels?"

"Well, they've loitered around in the past," he says. "It's not impossible one would try to see where the door would lead."

"Okay. I guess I scared 'em away, then."

"Maybe so. Preakle, make sure you play it smart around here. If you get to nosing around too much, Robbins will have both of us for lunch. As of yesterday, she was removed from my supervision and is now reporting directly to the superintendent."

"Does that make you two peers, then? Co-principals?"

"I don't know what the hell it makes us, Preakle. The superintendent hasn't been returning my calls the last few days, either. The sorry joker's probably avoiding me because he's too weak to can my sorry ass."

"Is that right?" I ask, appreciating his candidness.

"Preakle, if you haven't figured it out yet, I've got a laundry list a mile long of reasons to be fired. I guess there's just something endearing about this round, bald fellow."

I nod. "If Robbins is being groomed to succeed you, what's next?"

"Well, Preakle, that's part of what I'd like to talk to you about. With Hoblitz dead and gone, I'm going to be needing a new..."

"Lead custodian?" I interrupt.

"Well, yes. The role goes above and beyond just the basics, though. There are other duties I'll expect from you. It comes with a raise, of course."

"And my replacement?"

"I don't know yet," he says, chewing on his number two pencil. "What I know is there's a lot to be done around here and we shouldn't doddle around too much with a puppet like Robbins so close by."

"What kind of raise are we talking about?"

He keeps a straight face for a moment. "Preakle, I like you, and I appreciate your direct approach. How does three hundred a week sound? That's a fifteen grand a year raise, overnight. Not too shabby, huh?"

I shake my head, knowing that there's a lot more to this untimely "promotion" than working for the school and may or may not include activities that are illegal. Who knows? Whatever the hell it may entail leaves me convinces I'm in for a wild ride. This I'm certain of. I play down the question. Answering logically seems my best approach.

"Do you really have that kind of leverage? I don't mean to be skeptical, but I know government affairs require a lot of approvals to make big changes."

Fatts scoffs. "You work for me, Preakle, not the school. There are some questions you just shouldn't ask! Understand?"

"Yes, sir."

"Now, get on, and get to work!" Fatts says, the tension in his voice escalating as he slams the door.

I get through the day cleaning around the school. The kids and teachers go about their business just like they always do with occasional pointing and laughing, but nothing that I can't tolerate at this point. I tuck a few tools beneath my belt. There's a leak in the ladies' room on the east wing that needs fixing. Thankfully, no one's said anything. As I tighten up the leaking pipe, I wrap the connections crudely with plumber's tape and a misplaced dab of putty jammed beneath. I'm a crappy plumber, at best. The bathroom door creaks open, and the lights turn off. School's out for the day, so I'm not expecting anyone.

"Excuse me," I call out. "Custodian's in here. Please go to the west end restrooms and leave the lights on."

I'm about ready to go on heart pills. I can't take any more. If this ends up being some kid screwing around, I'll flip a lid. If it's a teacher, I may just flick a wrench at 'em and hope they drop dead. Either way, it won't be pretty. I hate being interrupted by stupid things like this.

"Of course, Pool Man," a voice calls through a megaphone. "Haven't you got higher priorities to tend to?"

Despite my best efforts, I can't ignore my nerves. Perspiration seeps from my forehead, and footsteps move closer. I peek under the stall to get a look, but they're average sized black tennis shoes, nothing conclusive. Their pants are all black, too. My wrench is ready for action.

"Your voice is a dead giveaway. I know who you are," I lie, tightening up the pipe's connection.

"I don't think so," the voice says, calling my bluff. "We'll make a hell of a team when we work together, Pool Man. You're welcome, by the way..."

"Welcome for what?" I ask.

"Getting rid of him for you. The job's all yours now."

The lights come back on, and the door squeaks and then closes, as the toilet leaks again and a stream of sweat runs down the back of my work uniform. I'm unable to differentiate whether the voice was male or female. I look down at my necklace, my reminder of Denny. I still keep it with me every day.

Easing back into the hallway slowly, I keep my pipe wrench cocked in the air as a potential mode of defense. A few other faculty and staff are still around for the day, but I'm unclear as to who might be taunting me. As I head to the basement, a voice calls out to me from down the hallway. It's Robbins.

"Mr. Preakle, do you have a moment?"

I nod, walking toward her.

"Please come into my office."

As we go into the room, she raises the blinds and peers out the window. "I want you to look down," she says, motioning to the sill.

"In the parking lot?" I ask.

"No. The window. Look at this. The dust... the dead flies... the old candy wrapper. A neglected toddler's habitat is cleaner after a week of mommy being gone than this window is right now. It's pathetic. I expect things done better."

"I understand."

I nod, seriously wondering if Mr. Fatts has clarified that Hoblitz's retirement was permanent, six feet under, and involuntary. Somehow, I doubt it.

"How long do you think this mess has been here?" she asks, her voice raising.

"Umm..."

"How long?!" she interrupts.

There's nothing more intimidating than an angry woman. And I mean nothing.

"A few weeks," I reply.

"Try years. I don't expect much, Greg, but this is basic stuff. Why don't you pay more attention?"

"I don't know. There's always so much to do. I just don't know where to start sometimes," I say, fishing a duster from the closet, dabbing some of the dust off the blinds with my finger.

"And what is your approach? Do you follow your checklists methodically?"

"Not really. I just like to move things along. You know, to come to a conclusion."

"And I suppose Principal Fatts is okay with this approach?" she asks, scoffing. "I saw him speaking to you earlier. I assume you know what's next for him? I expect more from you. If I don't get better results soon, there will be consequences."

"Yes, ma'am," I reply. "I'll bring the dust buster in every Thursday. I'll add it to my checklist."

"While you're at it," she mutters, "get those vending machines stocked up with granola bars. Empty the soda machines. I've heard they've started bottling water up lately. Let's get some of that. No more sugar in here... it's a silent killer."

I curl my lips. "Nobody wants to pay for bottled water. Most of us use the water fountains, ma'am. The bottled water isn't much a thing around here, and the vending machines are outsourced to an outside company."

"It will be! No debates, janitor. Figure out a way, please."

"Yes, ma'am."

She tucks her hands behind her back, clomping out of the room without a formal goodbye.

Despite a rougher day and some tough love from administration, my mind keeps wandering.

To Hoblitz and the slugs.

To Fatts and Dr. Hicks.

To the door in the basement.

To the harasser on campus, not to mention the one at home. I don't know if they are one and the same. They could be, then again, they may not be. There are coincidences, and there are connections, but where I get stuck is where coincidence and connection intersect—a collision of wit and will, and me standing dead center trying to distinguish the difference between the two.

It's all a little much.

Maybe I'm *too* aware. Too relaxed about it all of it. I need therapy, but I don't want to pay.

My mind's still racing. All this death, it's getting to me.

I scare myself thinking about a funeral.

The damn eulogy.

Oh, God. I'm not worthy of a violin player or a mourner. Just some melancholy preacher man behind a cheap-ass microphone that says, "This was Greg Preakle. A man that could have done more. A man that could have reacted to things. A man that went through the motions like a pre-programmed drone from beginning to end. That's it."

All four people in the audience nod their head, and there I am in the casket staring at the ceiling and nodding just the same, only along for the ride.

Oh, brother, get me some help.

The best way I can change is to be a part of it. And that's something I have to work on before these situations get any more out of hand. Where do I start, though?

CHAPTER TWENTY-TWO
NIGHTTIME SNOOP

I prep to leave campus for my evening break until another commotion in the basement grabs my attention from the top of the stairs. I move toward the source, going off the assumption that the noise originates from behind the unmarked door. It's a risk, but I'm willing to take it. I get into Hoblitz's drawer full of tools and pull out a heavy-duty screwdriver, hoping to pry it open with a little more force. Jamming it into the door, I wrench it around, the ongoing ruckus undoubtedly alerting any bystanders that may wait on the other side. As the door pops open slowly, I peer into what Fatts described as the "Tornado Shelter." I don't find that an accurate description. In fact, the room is lit well by what I assume is tied into the school's electrical grid. As for the room, it's unassuming. There's a chalkboard and a table with a few chairs around it. The board is freshly erased, its remaining chalk dust on the floor just beneath. There's a faint outline on the board. I can't quite make out what's left, but it appears to be a list. At the back of the room, there's another door. I walk toward it, keeping the large screwdriver in an attack position in case I'm caught snooping. From the looks of things, this door is used frequently. I open it slowly, moving across the room toward an operating table, a wall of scalpels, supplies, and medications. There's a set of doctor's medical scrubs hanging on the wall. I'm unclear what I've stumbled upon, but I'm assuming anyone that's practicing medicine in an unmarked basement tunnel attached to a school is unlikely to be performing anything... kosher.

In the back of the room, I notice a spiral with a bunch of scribbled notes and terminologies I don't follow, a couple of poster schematics with slugs on them. Some x's marked on human bodies. Medical and surgical terms and lots of arrows.

Before I can explore the area any further, the lights in the room turn off.

Damn. I'm caught.

I slip out through both rooms and into the basement quietly, pulling the door closed and making my best effort to mask evidence of tampering. After several minutes of tidying up around the basement, I leave the school, somehow avoiding a confrontation. I don't know if the lights were on a timer or if someone was sending me a message. Either way, I've got to watch myself a little closer.

I think it's time to take that break.

***

The miles across town click away as if I'm on autopilot. My mind's reeling on the basement space, what in the world happens in there, and why. I inhale a cheeseburger and gulp it down with some cold overcooked fries. Break's over.

The school comes into view, and I put the Ranger into park. As I prep to finish the last hours of my shift, I notice a black Towncar parked out front, backed into a space under a large oak tree. It might be the same one, but I'm not sure. I glance up at the school. The lights are on in the science lab again. It's uncommon for staff to work this late on typical weeknights. Most of them just take papers and tests home to grade them if they are running behind.

Upon entering the building, the lights at the far end of the hall flicker, leaving me on edge. I'm uneasy about the whole situation. As I've mentioned, I'm not an overly spiritual man, but I will say working alone in an old building has a certain weirdness to it. I'm a grown man. I've seen a lot, lived a lot, and suffered a lot, but this is different. The visitor obviously made themselves known parking out front, or maybe they're sending me a message. Then again, it could be a spouse's vehicle I'm just not accustomed to seeing. I go down the hallway on the defense, debating if I should check the science lab or leave it alone and get on with the evening shift. I walk back down into the basement and clock in. One of the showers is running. I shut the water off, and inspect the area. The basement's empty. Not only do I have a list of tasks to complete inside a short three-hour window, I've also got school resources wasting and leaving me the one to answer for them.

I move toward Fatts' office, cueing up my evening tunes on the intercom—Quiet Riot will help me close out the shift. Opting to go into the gym first, I flip on a slew of the room's light switches and start prepping the sweeper to wax the floor. As the lights take a few minutes to warm, I notice a floating silhouette on the far side of the gym and my breath loses rhythm. I let out an ugly gasp. The lights reach their optimum brightness, and that's when I see him.

"Dear God!" I call out.

I can't get any closer. It's too much to take in. Coach Rick Simmons, 41, husband and father of two, dangles from the basketball hoop—his mouth jammed into the iron rim and his whistle twisted in a knot of hair atop his scalp. The rim's drooping from the excess weight as a trail of blood seeps down his bare legs and a stack of twenty-dollar bills dangle from his mouth. I study the light's reflection on the blood, a pile of teeth, and a growing puddle of discharge on the ground just beneath. I lose it, retching and contaminating the otherwise untampered crime scene— further reiterating if I ever had made it to Vietnam, I wouldn't have been able to stomach the carnage.

A distorted voice calls from across the gym through a megaphone, dressed in all black and wearing a mask. "Dead and gone. Quite the pawn!"

I run across the room, struggling to get to the other side fast enough. I'm simply too jarred. Studying the long hallway corridor, no one loiters. The lights in the science lab are off now. Going back to the gym area, I'm overwhelmed.

Rick Simmons.

The husband.

The coach.

The father.

The jock.

"Dead and gone. Quite the pawn!" echoing through my mind through the distorted muffle of the megaphone.

God help me. I don't know. I owe it to his wife and children to call the cops, but at this point, I've got to be selfish and save my own hide. Whoever this freak is may still be in the building, and I can't take any chances. I decide to wait. I don't relish upon hanging so close to another corpse. There's an ugly pattern here, and

I don't want to be part of it anymore. Nobody's coming after me. There's no red laser on me yet. They could have left. I don't have to be a hero, though. It's one thing to take initiative. It's another to be a dumbass vigilante.

A few minutes go by, and I've yet to call the cops. I'm in shock. That's a valid excuse, right? There's a part of me thinking, if I just stay put and this goon's still in the hall, we won't have a confrontation that ends with me in a body bag.

My perch is several feet away from the body. That's as close as I'm getting. Don't think me a sociopath. I'm just a reluctant introvert that's not ready to die. I notice a trail of Tark slugs slithering across the floor toward his blood. A couple are already feasting.

"Oh, gosh! Get off him!" I say, kicking them away and across the room, Simmons' blood spreading everywhere. They must have gotten out of the science lab or the attic.

I head upstairs. The lock's been forced open to both the larger attic space and to the area that Fatts and Hoblitz called their own, the padlock tossed on the floor carelessly and clipped open with bolt cutters. The terrarium's knocked over and the room is ransacked. I dial 911 from the attic telephone. Another batch of Tark slugs crawls in a row toward the stairwell.

"Hi... um, yes, it's Greg Preakle, the custodian at the West Riverton High School. I'm here to report an incident."

The operator replies, "Yes, sir. What seems to be the issue?"

"One of our coaches is dead in the gymnasium," I reply, my breath escalating.

"I'm so sorry to hear that. Does it look like an accident? A suicide? What happened?" the operator asks.

"No. I don't think so. I came back from my evening break and found him. Whoever did this was trying to send a message. I'm just not sure to what or to whom!"

"I need you to remain calm, sir. Is there anyone else still in the school with you?"

"I saw someone in a mask. They taunted me and ran away before I could get over to them."

"Yes, sir. Could you tell if it was a man or woman? Any defining characteristics?"

I twist the phone cord around my finger. "They were all the way across the gym. I couldn't say. They were dressed in all black and yelled at me through a bullhorn, so whether male or female, I don't know. The voice was a middle range."

"Okay, sir. At West Riverton High School? And the victim's name?"

"Yes. It's Coach Rick Simmons."

"Okay, thanks. Are *you* safe? I need to make sure you're not in any danger."

"I don't know! Come on. Just send someone!"

"Calm down, sir! Keep the building secure until we get an officer there," the operator says, firmly. "And please don't touch anything until we get some help."

"I'm afraid," I say.

"Afraid of what?"

"That the body will collapse, and he'll splatter everywhere."

"What do you mean, sir?"

"It's dangling in the air. He's jammed into the basketball hoop."

"We'll send help as soon as possible."

Great. As soon as possible means "not anytime soon." I don't even know why I bother loitering at this point. I'm ready to just go home. If I wait around another hour, I'll be jammed on the rim on the opposite end in some kind of nutball's abstract art project. Listen to me getting more cynical by the day. I swear it's the job. Or something they're piping through the vents around here. Sheesh, listen to me starting to sound like my mother right before the end...

CHAPTER TWENTY-THREE
ALL CRACKED UP

Something deep within me cracks. Yep. Totally split in two. Another grisly death and I just can't cope anymore. No cops here yet, either. That's civil servants for you. I have nothing but respect for them, but this kind of delay is just unacceptable.

I tidy up the attic break room space, returning the neighboring Tark slugs to their terrarium and placing it upright. The tentacles on these guys is something to see. In this moment, I imagine Fatts' voice. "It's the euphoria. The rush. That adventure of going into the unknown..."

I'm done.

This is my moment.

I'm living for me.

Maybe it'll take the edge off.

Yeah. That's exactly what I need. No more edginess. I mean, honestly, I've never caved, not one single time. Never on any drugs. Just the beer, and never drunk, only buzzed. I think of hundreds of rock songs and stories about a life I'll never live. I've had a hell of a lot of self-control. It only takes a second to change, though.

I pick up the little fellow, bite its tail off and suck. Jubilation sets in, and I'm washed away into a milky haze, like something I've seen on an awful movie made for television, the edges of my eyes, wobbling and creamy. The attic break room is my playground now. Yes. What a playground.

There's a videocassette in the VCR deck that says "PLAY ME."

I turn it on. The footage is a step above amateur but poorly edited. It feels as if it's in slow motion, every detail jumping out in 3D. Maybe it's the slug, or perhaps it's the power of suggestion. It's all relative. I imagine the cops are pulling up now. They'll probably find me and pin the whole thing on me, and I'll forever be known as the janitor man that snapped. I don't care anymore. It's got to be the slug doing this. I'm not this dopey. My eyes are glued to the screen.

Coach Simmons jumps out of his vehicle, frazzled and pulling out keys to the building. He looks over his shoulder and runs inside the school. The camera pans to a black costumed voyeur staring at him from unmanicured bushes near the school's entrance. Coach moves into the building, seemingly oblivious to the fact that his stalker remains only a few steps behind. The camera cuts back to the stalker again, who slips in before the door clicks shut. Simmons jogs down the hallway toward his classroom.

"Greg? You on duty tonight?" he calls down the hall, only the hum of the school's air conditioner chirping back.

The one night I go out for a hamburger on my lunch break, this goes down. I'm starting to feel like Greenwich did with the floater by the pool, "shit out of luck with a dead man to answer for."

Simmons unlocks the science lab and lets himself in.

"I've got to get these tests graded," he says, more a poor actor than a teacher.

He pulls his desk drawer open, finds a bottle of liquor, and starts grading. A minute later, he jumps up—his impending needs leading him to piss in the drain in the middle of the lab. He scratches his butt and lets out a sigh. A flash reflects off the outside window.

He looks around for a minute, clearly thrown off. "Lightning, but no thunder? What the hell?" he mumbles.

What in heaven's name am I watching? Who made this?

Simmons zips back up and goes to his desk, continuing to grade as he chews a very worn red pen. A dribbling sound in the gym catches his attention. He gets up to inspect and enters the hallway. Firing up the lights in the gymnasium, there's a distant buzz and a rack of basketballs roll toward him in a rush. Their familiar bounces fetch his attention as a whistle blows. There's only the pale red glow of the room's scoreboard as the lights continue their warmup cycle. A dark figure moves across.

Looking down, he notes a wet stain on the front of his gym shorts. "Who's in here? School's closed!"

The stalker's voice chirps through a megaphone. "Should have locked up when you came in, Coach!"

"Who the hell is it?" he yells.

My heart's racing as I watch, my affectation for the slug rush gone just as fast as it came. Stupid choice. I've got to ride the wave... all the way up and all the way down.

"You better get over here and find out," the harasser taunts. "I got you on video... 'spraying' the science lab. How sanitary is that? A man of your seniority at the school should know better."

"Hold it!" he yells. "I'm sure we can come to an arrangement. What do you want from me?"

The lights in the room come up to full brightness.

"The rest of the money, Rick. You weren't fully vested."

"I should have known! I knew this whole ploy was a mistake," Simmons calls out.

The prowler rushes toward him. The video stops. Moments later, I'm back to my senses, more rational than I was before, much more cognitive, and facing a difficult truth. There's still a dead man in the building.

I walk down the stairs, wiping the brown goo stuck to my lips from the slug, and rinse my face in the hall bathroom. There's a commotion at the door as I come into the hall. I'm still under the influence of something... otherworldly, for lack of a better word. Making my way to the school's entrance, the sparkling red and blues grab my attention, and I pop the door open.

"Thank, God. It's good to see you guys here. Coach Simmons... is in the gym."

I extend my hand to shake the officers'. "I'm Greg Preakle."

"Detective Neil Penske. This is my partner, Abram Markel. It's a pleasure to meet you, Greg. I'm sorry about the circumstances, though."

"And, likewise, sir," Markel says.

I sigh. "Ditto. It's just down the hall here."

Penske nods. "Good. This sounds like another weird one, Abram."

"I would agree," I say as we walk through the corridor. "I was on my evening break and when I got back, I found Mr. Simmons."

"Thank you, Mr. Preakle," Penske says, pulling the doors to the gymnasium open. We're immediately hit with a growing stench. Penske stares me down, his frown shifting to disgust. Markel's seconds away from losing his Big Mac as Simmons decays. As we move closer, it's apparent that the skin on Simmons' face is sagging, almost to the point of melting right off his bones and onto the floor. Before we can get any closer, he slips from the rim and net and onto the ground.

CRASH!

The greater parts of his body spraying and splashing everywhere, an icky brown goo accompanying the bloodbath.

"Good freaking grief, we never catch a break, do we?" Penske says.

Markel stands shellshocked as he's covered in blood and guts.

"Always happens to the junior detective on duty. Sorry, Abram."

"It's a good thing this wasn't my Armani. Sheesh."

"A darn good thing. Wait... you can't afford an Armani," Penske replies.

"I do some moonlighting," Markle says, flecking some of the goo and blood from his jacket. "Mr. Preakle, don't feel you have to wait around. I know this is troubling. You can continue your duties if you're up for it. We don't want to keep school closed for too long. Too many parents will go psycho."

"Continue my duties? Are you kidding? Don't you have any more questions?" I ask.

"Well, I assume you would have told us if you knew more," Penske replies, jotting some notes in a small spiral. "You got back from your break, you witnessed the victim in his... position, and now you're a witness to how quickly the body decays. Anything else?"

"The killer wore black," I say. "They seemed to know their way around here."

"You saw them?"

"Just when I first found Simmons. They taunted me through a megaphone."

"That's right. The dispatcher mentioned that. You couldn't get over in time to subdue or stop them?"

I shake my head. "No, sir. I wish I could have."

"Anything else *meaningful* you wish to contribute?" Penske asks. "Any reason Simmons was here after hours or who else might have been here with him?"

"No, sir. Nothing that comes to mind."

"Alright. Have you notified administration?"

"Not yet, sir," I say.

"Since this happened on school property, they'll have to get involved. Unless you have reason to believe they're involved with the crime."

"Nothing's impossible, detective."

"Okay, well, I take it you're fine with a fingerprinting check? We need to rule you out as a suspect as well."

"That's not a problem, sir. I want to see that justice is served."

Penske nods. "One more thing, Mr. Preakle. You've got something stuck between your teeth. Some kind of brown goo."

"Thanks. Must have been the Chinese food I had earlier," I lie. "That's embarrassing. Thanks, officers. Good luck."

"Thank you, Mr. Preakle. We'll be in touch."

I move down the hallway as sweat rolls down my neck from the evening's trying events. As I dab the back of it, a bit of brown goo seeps from my pores. That'll teach me to think twice about sucking slugs. A far worse side effect than beer breath.

***

I haven't left the school yet. I'm surprised the police haven't kicked me out. At this point, the bizarre high from the Tark slug seems to have dissipated. I think the effects have mostly worn off but I can't say for sure.

Detective Penske's standing in the hallway with Principal Fatts.

We make eye contact as he speaks. "Hello, Mr. Preakle. I sent Officer Markel home to change clothes. Principal Fatts has just given us his statement, so we're prepping to wrap until we get back into the daylight hours. Is there anything else around here that was tampered with or altered that you noticed in your evening checks?"

Fatts looks at me in a way that says, "the less I say, the better."

I don't know what the guy's up to. I never have. I'm more and more convinced this entire mystery's just going to unravel like an ugly knitted Christmas sweater. I just hope I have the last laugh.

"Nothing really, detective," I reply.

Penske nods. "Gentlemen, please see that the school is locked up and closed until further notice. I suspect we'll be able to get things back in business by the end of the week and just close the gymnasium down at that point for security measures."

"Makes sense to me," Fatts says.

"Whatever we can do to curb the issue is priority one," I interject.

As we peer outside the window, a slew of vans, cameras, and crews stand there waiting for us.

"Detective? Who notified the press?" Fatts asks.

"I don't think it was any of us. We don't want word of this thing getting out too quickly. Otherwise, we end up going on public record, and giving a lot of detail to more people than necessary. My advice to you, gentlemen, find another way out, and hitch a ride."

"We can slip out the basement door on the far side," Fatts replies.

"Great. I'll follow behind," Penske says. "I'm not ready for a press conference, either. I've got to get my hair parted just right."

Fatts nods. "I'll notify the press of tomorrow's closure, and get in touch with AP Robbins as well," he says. "I didn't see a need to bring her up here tonight, but she needs to be debriefed about the situation for her own safety. Preakle, I'm sorry you had to see that. It must have been an awful scene. Simmons put in a lot of hours here. He sure burned the midnight oil for those kids," he says, sniffling, a tear going down his cheek.

We move into the basement, each of us slipping out of the building and heading our separate ways for the night. I walk across the grass, finding my way to the bus to hitch a ride home. I don't want to pay the fare, but the truck's in the parking lot next to the commotion out front, so I'll catch up with it tomorrow.

CHAPTER TWENTY-FOUR
LOSING MY WAY

I wake in the storeroom closet of the school, lost in a haze, and feeling out of control. Hoblitz comes out of the corner, a hazy smoke and yellowish tint following behind.

"You know what you need to do. I took too long," he says.

I know he's not there. It can't be him. I can't let this happen. I pull out a Tark slug from my shirt pocket and suck it fast. The stress melts away, and that's when the image plays out in front of me. The perfect way to clean up the mess around here. I come out of the hall closet and hear the familiar clomping from the east end of the building. I follow behind with my squeegee and bucket, a trail of water rolling down the floor.

"Excuse me, AP Robbins," I say. "I wanted to bring something to your attention. I'd like a senior staff member's advice."

"I don't have all day, Mr. Preakle. What's so important that you're interrupting my normal duties?" she asks, squinting her eyes at me. "What is that coming out of your forehead? That brown goo?"

"Oh, just some oil or something from the shop," I lie, wiping it off. "Don't worry. I'll tend to it later."

"So, what is it you need?"

I sigh, studying the small wrinkles under her eyes. "Umm... I saw some students hanging around in here. School's closed for the day, and I don't want to handle it on my own."

"Well, I'll come with you, then," she says. "I'm always in the mood to discipline—even when I'm off duty. It's my therapy. Heh."

What a sick thought. We round the corner to a dark part of the hallway where there is a red exit sign. I've put off fixing the sign and its exposed wires until now. I think back to the night I found mom dead on the floor, and something just snaps, my resentment launching me into uncontrolled mania.

Who is Robbins? An appointed female authority figure.

Who was mom? An inherited female authority figure.

Their tracks run parallel in my simple mind. It skews my perception of all female authority figures. It's unhealthy, and it's wrong, probably even the reason I never got serious with a woman. Trust issues. Years and years of them.

I make eye contact with Robbins. She's strikingly good-looking. It's a pity she's so pinned up. I'm coming unhinged.

"Umm... I need a favor, ma'am," I say, looking up and down either side of the hallway.

"Go on," she says, her patience wearing thin. "What can I do? Where are the students?"

"They must have gone behind the door in the electrical closet. I need to tend to this first, though... Do you mind... uh... bringing that ladder over there under the exit sign? I think there's a short in the wire."

She scoffs, grabbing at her pantsuit and dropping her hand on her hip. "And why can't you do this? Oh... that's right... your arm. Tch. I didn't kiss butts in graduate school for nothing, Mr. Preakle. I've wanted to be on top for a while. It's not my fault our principal played tiddlywinks one time too many with that redheaded whore and got caught."

I shake my head, walking across the room toward the ladder. "I just want to show you how I handle this type of situation. You know, so you can appreciate what I do a little more."

She squints her eyes at me, moving the ladder beneath the unlit sign. "Appreciate? Okay? Fine. What can I do?"

"Thanks. Just wait there in case I need a spotter. I don't want the ladder to topple," I call out.

I climb up and fidget with the sign. AP Robbins stares up at me, growing more curious by my methods.

"Such sloppy work, Greg."

Looking back at her, her pronounced nose and squinty eyes trouble me. I imagine her clogs traipsing through the hallway.

CLOMP. CLOMP. CLOMP.

And then I think of our jobs.

I've had enough. Fishing the live wire from the ceiling, I lower the exit sign toward the floor.

"Were you luring me back here, Greg? What do you want with me?" she asks, running her fingers through her dyed blonde hair.

"You assume I'm trying to come on to you because we're in a dark hallway?" I ask, scoffing. "You're no Cindy Crawford," I say. Robbins is prettier.

Simmons comes in behind her, mimicking a throat slitting motion. A red and blue hue shines on him in the corner, his discombobulated body glued back together. He's not there. I'm just off my rocker, going batshit nuts.

"Excuse me? What did you say? Are you harassing me?" she asks, tapping her foot on the floor.

I see myself falling from the bars again, my career with the military over before it could ever take off... it eats me up inside. The clomp, clomp, clomp as she walks away sets me off.

"Hold it!" I yell, lunging across the room, grabbing her by the throat, and yanking her close. She gags as I jam the live wires from the exit sign into her mouth and her face lights up. There's a brief pop from the moisture on her tongue as it makes contact with the electricity. She drops to the floor. I look down the hallway. Hoblitz hobbles toward me, an ugly grin on his face.

What have I done?

I stare at her wide eyes, frozen in time, and wondering if she's really dead. I've got to do something before someone else sees the mess.

Finding the breaker box, I cut the power and emergency auxiliary lines to this wing of the school and tuck the leather work glove I'm wearing into my pocket. I yank the wires from her mouth.

There's a disgusting part of me satisfied with the outcome.

Nobody liked her.

Nobody will miss her, either.

Hoblitz and Simmons come toward me, clapping and smiling. I can't hear the sound.

If I save Fatts' job, I save my own. It's the logical solution. I wrap the wires around her neck and plop her on the floor. There aren't many that would suspect a suicide, but rather than risk getting caught hiding the body, staging a death under these circumstances seems the best way to minimize suspicion.

***

My eyes pop open as I awake on the bus just outside Cove Ridge. The old man driving the bus looks at me and points. "You got some brown goo on you there, fella."

"Oh, gosh," I say, wiping it off and chuckling. "Well, this is my stop. I guess it's time for a shower. Got a little messy at work today.

Good grief. What a mess.

Robbins isn't dead, and I'm not a killer. Thank God. I'm reminded why giving up control is a hard thing for me. It's too unpredictable. I rinse off in the shower, more goo seeping from my pores.

I hate these lines that keep blurring my realities and my nightmares, washing one another out and taking me further and further away from the man I need to be. The man I want to be. As the water from the shower streams down my skin, I see the electricity coursing through Robbins again just like the dream. Whether an idealized thought, or a terrible side effect of my Tark slug abuse, I'm unclear. I dry off and study the bathroom mirror. It's foggy. And I guess that's about what I am, too.

CHAPTER TWENTY-FIVE
NIGHTLY NEWS

It's not tasteful to admit this, but by my count, it's been twenty hours since I sucked.

I had the day off with the school closed. I flipped channels for hours, went through another six-pack, and rearranged my dresser a couple of times. Simmons is still dead. And so is Hoblitz. I remember the list in Fatts' office. They were both on it. I start to consider that I may be next. If there is any sort of M.O. for this killer, I don't quite see the pattern other than a common place of employment. Simmons was a chump, yes, but that doesn't tell me why someone wanted him dead. Certainly not as dead as he was. If there's one thing seeing a few dead bodies has taught me, it's that there are degrees to deadness.

To hell in a handbasket, to the moon and back, or just a rock's throw away in the cemetery behind grandma's house.

What am I saying? Who am I talking to?

I've got to get out of the house to clear my head. I'll roll the windows down, take in the evening air, enjoy some loud music, and block out the rest.

It's not that easy. I keep thinking.

My dream of killing Robbins.

Of Simmons' grisly death.

Of Hoblitz's untimely demise.

I completely blanked out about the videotape I found in the attic. I suppose the cops will find it eventually if they're thorough enough. I shouldn't have crossed into the slug sucking arena— a slippery slope to a netherworld where I'm neither welcomed nor shunned.

The tape plays in my mind again. The prowler waiting in the bushes, the black garb and their graceful movements like some kind of house cat after hours—a real mischief maker with refined skill. It's cold. It's calculated. And it's personal, almost always personal.

I go outside and jump in the truck.

Poison blares through the speakers. One song. Then two. Then three. Hell of an A side. I've got one of those fancy cassette decks that flips over on its own.

Somehow, the drive takes me to the last place I want to be as I breeze past my former employer and its fresh blacktop.

Those sorry S.O.B.'s!

Castle Productions is just a few lots down and it's the point of origin to most of my problems. There's always been something to the area that's left me uneasy. As I drive by, I see Fatts come out of the building talking with a spastic and animated fellow with bleached blonde hair. I don't know why I feel the need not to be seen, but I'm crossing my fingers there's no realization that I'm nearby. I don't want them to see. I cruise on by, hoping Fatts doesn't recognize the Ranger.

Who am I kidding? Of course he does. It's hard coded in a man's DNA to know this kind of stuff.

Is it more conspicuous not to stop or coincidentally be in the same area and act oblivious? He's too lost in conversation to pay attention to me. That plastered smile on his face is probably influenced by a lot of slug sucking and booze. I'm too far off to hear what they're saying, though.

I shake my head, biting my lip. It's a self-awareness quirk, I guess. I can't keep running. I've got to get some answers. I need resolution. If this guy really is the source of my woes, perhaps the best thing I can do to dodge him and still find my way is snoop when he's not looking. No risk, no reward. Or incarceration for life, depending on if I get caught.

I circle around, staking out the studio just down the block. I pull out an old pack of cigarettes from the glove box. I haven't smoked in years, but they've been there waiting for the right moment. I can taste them, feel the burn long before I ever pull the cancer stick out from the crackling wrapper. That familiar smell. It makes me think of mom. That's why I gave them up. It hurts too much. I've swapped cassettes from Van Halen to Def Leppard two times over now, just hoping and waiting for that beat-up blue Cutlass Ciera to move on so I can take a closer look and check out the studio a little more. At this point, I'm assuming when he leaves, Fatts will, too. I recall the *Twisted Hacks* tapes in the attic at the school, too, which he seemed enthusiastic about. The other guy is strikingly familiar. I just can't place him.

What does Fatts have to do with Castle Productions? Who is the other guy?

Fatts climbs into the vehicle with the other man, and they drive away. The faint glow of dim lights from the studio building shines through the front windows. It's now or never. I go up to the glass door and yank the handle. The door's locked. It's got one of those realtor padlocks on it that takes a combination. I peek inside. No one in the lobby. I look down at the lock again. It's jammed.

Am I really that lucky?

I check over my shoulder. Coast looks as clear as it's going to get. I yank at the padlock and the key drops onto the ground, its clinking echoing. I bend over and grab it. If I am seen, as best as I've got it figured, the best thing I can do is look confident and slip inside.

If I get caught, I'll just say I'm a realtor. Yeah. Jimmy Herald, realtor from Barton Hills. I've got an interested tenant. I don't know if that's going to fly. There's nothing in the window yet, but the padlock has me wondering.

I let myself inside. I'm not assuming anything, though. Someone may be in here and I have to be nimble. I look around the lobby. It's strangely empty. The receptionist's desk is gone. There are only a few chairs on the north wall. I see a FOR LEASE sign at the back of the room. That explains the realtor padlock. I'm kind of surprised. Castle Productions and Channel 33 have shared this building for years. They're not synonymous with one another, but they're certainly partners as Castle Productions programming is featured on it.

I go down the hallway in the lobby and find some offices in the back. If there's anything juicy, offices are where it would be. There's an office marked Studio Director and to its right is the Station Manager's office. Station Manager sounds more powerful. More power equals more information. Or that's what I'm inclined to think at this point. I doubt it's unlocked. Nope. No dice, no bright light coming beneath the door, just the faint glimmer of a computer screen, some kind of blue mainframe.

I notice a mail slot on the wall to the right of the doors. There are a few names.

D. Jones.

F. Wilks.

T. Garcia.

L. Fatts.

There's a piece of mail in the L. Fatts slot. I slide it out of the envelope and take a peek.

Lynette Fatts-Station Manager

Mrs. Fatts,

This note is to confirm the sale of your existing 51% stake in Castle Productions. Please contact me at your earliest convenience so we can complete the handoff.

My associates and I are looking forward to the big cutover later this year.

Sincerely,

Jason Rivas

Director, The Nightmare Channel

4248 Sunset Boulevard

Los Angeles, California, 42012

This thing just gets more and more interesting. I can't help but grin. A path down the rabbit hole. Hop little bunny, hop, hop, hop.

I move toward the studio area. I want to confirm my suspicions. This place must be real. They really do sever limbs, tear scalps, and worse. They're just living behind the guise that it's phony. It's fiction. Maybe I'm still crashing down from the Tark. What the hell is the half-life on this thing? Every time I think I'm on the downer, I'm back upper. I've got to stop this mother goose crap, stat. God wants me to.

There's a rattling sound. Someone's at the front door outside, rifling through their keys. Shit. Glancing down the rear corridor, I see an exit at the end of the hallway. I race down. It's shadowy enough back there to convince me I'm in the clear. I get over to it as the door pops open. I look down at the long bar handle. EMERGENCY EXIT ONLY.

What now?

Do or Die.

Hide out and hope you don't get caught.

Push the fire door and make yourself known.

Your fingerprints on everything.

The cops spotting your truck down the block, out of place.

Screwed no matter what.

The realtor gag. *Could it work?*

Depends on who the person is. I've been in here before. I'm a familiar face. I bolt out of the emergency exit. The alarm tripping and ringing through the building and the alley. A hefty woman screams at me from inside. She's yelling swear words at me. I don't hear the swearing anymore when it's a woman. I just tune it out and replace it with a bunch of euphemisms. Her scratchy voice comes out like an annoying out of towner. "You better stop right now before I pull out my blankity-blank gun, Mr. Blankity-blank blank blank!"

No, thanks. Not tonight.

I rush down the alleyway, faster than any wildcat I've ever seen, my heart racing, and praying no bums are witness to me. My arm's a dead giveaway.

I get around the corner. The Ranger's still there. I try to calm myself down, hoping to God that no one else saw me. The hefty woman inside was too slow.

If that doesn't get your blood pumping, I don't know what will.

I cruise down the block at normal speed. No music, no smokes. I can't right now. I'm not nosy; I swear, just a concerned citizen. I find it rather ironic that a television studio doesn't have any surveillance cameras. I guess the money goes into all the productions themselves. It's back home for the night. A few cold ones are waiting for me, assuming I'm not trailed by someone else. At this point, anything goes.

***

I head across town to Cove Ridge. Arriving home, I check over my shoulders to make sure no suspicious characters or onlookers are waiting and go into the house.

I turn the television on. Channel 33 rarely airs a news report, but there's a replay on. I guess the Simmons case is big enough for them to report on it. The news anchor speaks in a serious tone. "A teacher and coach at the West Riverton

High School was pronounced dead this morning after a janitor allegedly made the discovery and phoned it in to authorities. Here's Stoney Bleaker at the scene for this special breaking news report."

"Yes indeed, Bill. This is an unnerving situation. For Rick Simmons, it was just another day at the grind, pushing himself to make ends meet, and grooming the West Riverton Spartans for their first victory of the season. KVTL spoke with his wife, Edna, earlier today."

The tears of Mrs. Simmons trickle down the sides of her cheeks and she struggles to get the words out to Stoney. "I... I'm just not sure. He left today with mismatched socks and a grody coffee thermos just like any other day. I just... can't believe he's gone."

"Do you have any thoughts about who might be responsible?"

"I don't. He was..." she sniffles, "he was not a favorite around town. I'm not living under any delusions. Coaching high school sports to a losing team gets you in bad graces with a lot of people."

"Mrs. Simmons, are you inferring that a disgruntled player or parent could have done this?" Stoney asks.

"It's possible. I... I just don't know. I can't handle any more questions. Get the cameras out of here!"

The report switches back to Stoney on site at the school. "So, though we were abruptly cut short, I'm convinced that despite differences or marital struggles between the two, it's unlikely Mrs. Simmons is involved. Standing with me here now is Detective Neil Penske."

Penske nods as Principal Fatts loiters just behind. "Yes, I... uh... don't have a lot to say. This is not an official press conference. We are looking into the matter and hope to have school back in session as soon as possible."

Bleaker nods, "And gentlemen, do either of you have reason to think the janitor providing the tip is involved?"

"It's too early to say," Penske replies. "He's probably watching the report now like the rest of the town is, I'm sure. We've told him and several others to stay within an arm's length, but I have no reason to think he's involved at this phase."

Bleaker shakes his head. "I'm sorry, and what makes you think the guilty party wouldn't just run?"

Penske scoffs. "Too obvious. They want to seem cozy and unphased— to blend in with the rest. We're still weighing out our options. Nothing's cut and dry, and no one's ruled out entirely... except for Coach Simmons. Sparing you the grisly details, there's no way *this* death was self-inflicted."

"Well, we're out of time and have to cut to a commercial. Special thanks to Principal Fatts and Detective Penske. I'm Stoney Bleaker for KVTL. We'll bring you more on the story as it develops. Back to you in the studio, Bill."

"Thanks Stoney."

I click the television off, grab a Flitz, and step outside for some fresh air. Joan looks to be doing the same as she sits on her patio in her baby blue "couch potato" pajamas. She extinguishes her cigarette as she stares across the lot at me. It annoys me that our front doors face each other, but it's no easy feat to turn one of these things around.

"Did you see that bit on the news... about that coach?" she says, smoke coming out her nose and mouth concurrent to one another— her lazy Siamese cat hopping into her lap.

"Yeah. It was a mess."

"It's a real shame. Family man like that must run with the wrong crowd, huh? Speaking of... You... uh, had any more trouble with the man in the black car?"

"Not at this point," I reply, sipping on my beer. "I think that's been put to bed."

"How's that?" she asks, pulling out another cigarette and lighting it.

"It's like anything, Ms. Joan. They just want money. Probably just some goof off at the cable studio that's too lazy to find an actual job."

"I saw your episode the other night. I recognized your voice, 'Gregory.' They took your money?"

"Nine grand worth," I reply, nodding. "What's left of it's getting me by in the meantime."

"Well, spend it on something nice. You've been dealt a tough hand."

"No shit," I call out, raising my nub in the air. "Bad pun, though"

"Oh, sorry, Greg," she says, jabbing her cigarette on the side of the porch railing.

I wave her off. "I got to get to bed. Have a good night."

I head inside. Before I can get comfortable, my phone rings. As I pick it up, a strained voice comes on the line, "Greg, it's AP Robbins. I need someone to talk to. Can you meet up with me at the Perk-a-Lator?"

"This seems a little out of nowhere? What's going on? Are you okay?" I ask.

"I'm fine, but we need to meet."

"I'm sorry. I'm just a little thrown off hearing from you. Isn't the coffee shop closed?"

"Greg, it's 8:30. They're open until 10."

"Alright. I'll meet you there in about 15 minutes. That should give us an hour to discuss whatever you're wanting to meet about."

"See you then," she says.

I hang up the phone and sigh. I never gave her my number, so she's either tracking me through the phone book or school personnel records. Either way, it's a little odd. As for the day, I'm completely spent, but for Robbins and to keep my job, I'll make the time. As out of place as this encounter is and with all other things considered, I'm not really sure what to expect.

CHAPTER TWENTY-SIX
UNEXPECTED MEETING

I arrive at the Perk-a-Lator. The crooked parking job will have to do. Heading inside, I look around for Robbins. There's no sign of her. I request a black decaf coffee. It rarely takes much to keep me satisfied. I find my way to one of the back corner booths where a brick wall's exposed. There's a guy close by picking a guitar messily and I can only assume he's either related to the owner or free. What I'm trying to say is, the fact that I could give him a run for his money with one arm is laughable. I sip my coffee. It's stale, an obvious inferiority to its caffeinated sibling.

I study the room again, looking for a familiar face. AP Robbins is in the booth just behind me. She's just too short for me to see her over the top of it. I walk over toward her.

"Hello, Mr. Preakle," she says.

"Hi." I sit down and study her. She's fidgeting, and clearly not wanting to be here. I have no plans to drag this out.

"How are you?" she asks.

I sigh. "I don't know. How should I be?"

"That's about the answer I was expecting. As much has happened lately with our crazy boss, I just needed someone else level headed to talk to."

"I don't know that I'm at my most level-headed at this point," I mutter, sipping on my coffee.

"Well, that's all subject to whatever crazy moment we're in, isn't it?" she says, matter-of-factly.

"What's up, then?" I say. "I've got no qualms about meeting. But this does seem a little... unexpected."

She nods. "It is. And I tried racking the brains of a few others on staff, but no one else seems to want to shoot straight with me. I guess I'm too intimidating."

"It's always an adjustment with a new person in charge," I reply. "It'll come with time."

"Mr. Preakle, since you're still new to the school, I want to discuss something that I'm at the school to review right now, but I ask you to keep this in the highest of confidences," she says, her voice dropping to a whisper as she checks over both shoulders.

Something feels a little off about the situation. I just sense it. "Okay? I'm all ears."

As I look her in the eyes, I struggle not to see her electrified face.

"Greg, Principal Fatts has been coercing staff members at West Riverton High in unsavory ways," she says, taking a drink.

"Oh? What do you mean?"

"I mean..." AP Robbins drops her head into her hands. When she looks up again, it's flush white.

"Ma'am, are you okay?"

She collapses, gagging and convulsing on the floor.

"Someone call 911!" I yell.

In a matter of sixty seconds, AP Robbins has flatlined. As authorities arrive upon the scene, she's pronounced dead, and I'm again tortured by an unsavory death inches away.

The coffee shop owner approaches the police and medics at the scene. "It's a good thing you ordered decaf. I caught the back door flung wide open earlier. My staff said there was a guy acting kind of strange in here. Someone they didn't recognize in a blonde wig."

Detective Penske comes through the door. "Mr. Preakle, we meet again."

"Yes, we do," I reply. "I didn't sign up for this."

"And here we are with yet another dead body, the common denominator... you."

"I swear on my mother's grave, I have nothing to do with this."

"We'll have the coffee tested," Penske says. "The Perk-A-Lator's lucky no one else came in tonight and the guitar player's hypersensitive to caffeine. What were you doing here with AP Robbins?"

"I don't know. Just take me in already. Put us all out of our misery, man."

"Why do you say that?"

"I received a phone call. She asked if I could meet. We only sat down together a moment ago. I ordered my decaf, and just as she started to open up, she keels over. She mentioned something about Principal Fatts and coercion. Next thing I know, she's gagging and gone."

"Hmm..." Penske says, taking some notes on his pad. "Nice and neat little story there. You want me to put a bow on it for you?"

I shake my head. "I just want to get on with my life without seeing anyone else lose theirs."

"You mentioned Principal Fatts. Have you seen or talked to him much outside of our talks?"

"As a matter of fact, I did. He was over there near the Castle Productions studio. I saw him on the news report with you, too."

"That's right. The news report. I'm short on sleep, Preakle. Forgive me. Did you stop and chat with him at the studio?"

"No. I didn't feel it appropriate at the time. He was with another man."

"Just between us, that Channel 33 and Castle Productions, they're into some dodgy business, Mr. Preakle."

As AP Robbins is taken away on a gurney, I'm escorted to Penske's unmarked patrol car.

"You know, us taking you in. It's just a matter of dotting the I's and crossing the T's," he says, putting me in the back seat. "We'll run you through the system, get another statement out of you, and let you go in the morning."

"I don't know," I reply. "A few nights in the lockup might be a good thing. I don't want anyone else around town to end up dead."

***

The Precinct Three station is an eyesore. I won't bore with the details. Government and municipal money around Riverton seems to go everywhere but the places that need it the most. I'm sitting in Penske's office. He has a box of case files at least two feet high and marked "unsolved." He swigs on his coffee and I cringe.

"I'm sorry," he calls out. "Would you like some?"

Of course I don't. I'm about to just snap. How insensitive can you be?

"I don't think so," I say. "Considering what just happened, I don't want any of it."

"Yeah. The tox screen just came in."

Cut to the chase and tell me. I'm out of steam.

"That was fast."

Penske nods. "These lab techs and their computers, they're quite a phenomenon. She was poisoned with an inordinate amount of arsenic. We don't see as much of that anymore. It's like a crime of yesteryear."

I nod. "Sounds about right."

Penske studies me closely for a moment and reviews his notes. "Mr. Preakle, have you had trouble around your place lately? Harassers? Threats? That kind of thing."

"A little. It just goes with living in a rough part of town, I reckon."

"A bit of a nonchalant response, don't you think?"

"I don't know," I reply, shaking my head. "I'm kind of numb to feelings. It's been really tough lately."

Penske scoffs. "Mr. Preakle, it's time we cut the crap and get right to the point."

"Oh?"

"We've been running surveillance near your place for a while. I've had a few of my guys out and about, monitoring how things operate in Cove Ridge. It's less about you and more about the area itself and its troubles. It's mostly boring trailer trash nonsense— some crystal meth here, a little heroin there, a couple of domestic battery cases. Otherwise, not all that eventful, but you don't match up with the rest of 'em. Your record's a little *too* clean. Until two weeks ago, when you accepted dirty money and took a job working at the school for Mr. Fatts."

"Dirty money? What do you mean?"

"Mr. Preakle, I want you to come across town with me," he says.

"Okay?"

We walk out of the station, and I'm loaded into Penske's vehicle. As we drive toward the Oak Hollow District, Penske speaks to me from the front seat. "Yeah. We got a tip that you were sitting on 10 Gs."

"What's this about? Where are you taking me?"

"I've been digging around, Mr. Preakle."

I shake my head. "I don't follow."

We pull into the lot next to the Castle Productions building. A "For Lease" sign sits in the window.

"I don't understand," I mutter. "Where is everything?"

"They started cleaning it out. Don't think they're completely done yet. I've got a warrant to search the premises. Markel will join us shortly to assist. I want to show you something. Look, there's the realtor pulling up now."

A beat-up Cutlass Ciera pulls up behind us and the bleached hair weirdo I saw with Fatts jumps out near the facility. He's quirky and a little spastic at first glance, and busy slurping on a large fountain drink.

"Hey, buddies. Buddies," he calls out. "Hey... Hey... I'm Johnny Lathrop. Pleased to meet you fellows. Take one of my cards. Take two!"

Penske extends a hand and shakes Johnny's. "I'm Detective Penske. This is Greg Preakle, a recent contestant."

"Yeah! Yeah! I saw that one. Gregory, right? It's hard to know with the helmet."

"Had a lot of caffeine tonight, Johnny?" Penske asks.

"You could say that," he says, pulling the key from his pocket and unlocking the building. "Come on in. Let's take a look. I'm always looking to help out lawmen, however I can."

At this moment, I'm convinced that Johnny's akin to a pesky rat. We walk through the lobby. The sun-stained walls where the Castle Productions signage once stood are bare. He walks us back into the main studio room and the circular seating area. Trickles of corn syrup are stained all over the floors. There are a few dangling prop appendages, even the whimsical spinning wheel I stood upon to answer questions. The audience is still as full as it ever was.

"I don't understand," I say, looking at the room.

Johnny walks over, removing the mask from one of the audience "members." It's faceless rubber.

"They're all mechanically operated dummies and mannequins. It was all part of the masquerade," he says.

"Castle Productions pulled the plug on a live audience a while back," Penske says. "Or so we're told. Only essential personnel and contestants. A lot of cued sound effects, flashing lights, and spinning floors kept everyone distracted."

"I could have figured," Lathrop says, chuckling, "the fake blood and arm and leg chops were a real trip. I swear they made you think it was real every time. Got to love TV. He-he. No offense, mister. Did you lose your arm in the line of duty?"

"Something like that," I mutter, his hap hearted insensitivity testing me. "All I can say is, when I was on the show, it seemed real."

"Why are they selling?" I ask. "They've been a staple to the local cable market for years."

"I'm not clear on that. They didn't tell me." Johnny replies, scratching at the back of his head.

"Who are they? The owners of the building?" I ask.

"Castle Productions," Penske replies.

"No," I interrupt. "What's the owner's name?"

"You mind?" Johnny asks, lighting up and taking a drag of a cigarette. "It's the fat man. Yeah, they call him Fatts. I've done odd jobs for him for years. A real renaissance man. His wife always handled the business side over here. He's kept it funded from other private ventures."

As I study the man a second longer, it dawns on me. I remember the realtor. He was the OIC that told us about Denny.

"Odd jobs?" I say. "I remember you. You served in 'Nam, right?"

He hesitates. "Uh, yeah. That's right."

"My brother was Denny Preakle. He was in Vietnam with you... in your unit. Remember him? You told us about him, about his death."

His eyes take a second to register as if his mental Rolodex has been fried by too many happy-hours. "That's right. Denny Preakle. I knew you looked familiar. I'm sorry."

"It's alright."

We walk toward the front of the building. I notice another door off to the side. "What's back there?"

"Oh, it's the stairs leading into the basement," Lathrop says. "We can go down if you want. I never hear of anything good happening in basements, though. So, if you'd rather not, I get it."

Penske nods. "Let's go have a look."

Officer Markle enters the building as Lathrop unlocks the door to the basement.

"Evening, guys. Sorry I'm late."

"No problem," Penske says. "As long as you have that vanilla latte I asked for, we're good."

"You got it, boss man," his energetic face, a little peculiar given the circumstances of the scenario.

"Has anyone ever told you how annoying you are?" Penske asks.

"I guess not," Markle says, his enthusiasm flattening.

I look over at Lathrop. He looks antsy, probably sipped too much of his soda and needs to relieve himself. He's teetering on annoying, but I'll tolerate him considering his service alongside of Denny. "Well, let's get down there, gentlemen," he calls out.

"You have *my* interest piqued," I reply.

As we enter the area, I notice a few lounge chairs, a ping-pong table, and a small bar with neon cocktail signs and a few 777 flashers near unplugged slot machines. The room reeks of sin, death, and greed.

"Just penny slots. Nothing illegal here, officers, ha-ha," Lathrop says, his chuckle a bit on the nervous side.

"Whatever," Penske says, jotting a few notes on his pad.

"Yeah, I hear this is where Fatts and 'the host'... entertained the ladies before and after the show," Lathrop says, grinning. "That host... he was something else. It was all a charade for the cameras, though. There's the 'SLIDE INTO CASH' slide. It let out just over there."

I shake my head. "I rode the slide. This doesn't look the same. I never came down here."

"Memory can be a tricky thing, Mr. Preakle," Penske replies. "Are you sure?"

"No, no. You're both wrong," Lathrop says, stroking his chin. "It's a double-decker slide. You remember? You go up the stairs, slide down, and land in the bathtub. There's a trapdoor under it that lets you come all the way down here, but that was only when the winner was more on the attractive side of things."

I nod. "Okay. That makes a little more sense."

"I guess you weren't worthy of the hideaway," Lathrop replies. "Your hips weren't quite contoured enough, were they? One of you guys want to ride it all the way down from the top?"

"Officer Markle does," Penske replies.

"You got it! That's right up my alley!" Like an overexcited puppy, the junior detective runs up the stairs.

Penske puffs air through his lips. "I've got to get this kid on decaf."

As we look at the orange slide, we hear Markle's excited yell as he comes down. "It's as slick as ever! Woo!" He comes out of the slide, an oversized grin on his face. "What a trip!"

"Mr. Lathrop, go take a smoke break or something," Penske says. "Get some fresh air."

"You don't have to tell me twice. It's happy hour at Bridgewater!" he says.

I knew it. The guy reeked of booziness the second I saw him.

Penske looks at me. "Mr. Preakle, we need to get some things straightened out. This whole thing's crooked. You were solicited by Castle Productions. You came in, filmed an episode, and were disbursed a sum of ten thousand dollars for your 'supposed' victory."

"I'm just a guy that fell on hard times. What's this got to do with me?" I ask.

"The money being circulated through town from Castle Productions is dirty. The winners are hand-picked, and the losers are spit out and left to rot. Mr. Preakle, I'm going to give you a second to get your thoughts together, and we can talk this through a little more."

"I signed a waiver," I say, a growing unease in my voice. "I was reassured that this was all legal."

Penske scoffs. "This is much bigger than a few crooks at a small-time game show, and we both know it. You know, greed can really ruin a man."

There's a less than silent whoosh and Penske collapses to the floor, a bullet coming out his right temple and into the wall just behind. A dark figure emerges from the corner of the room as another door swings open into a nearby tunnel.

A voice comes through the megaphone. "The thing about the silencer on the gun is that it's rarely silent at the scene. Especially once a two-hundred-pound body crashes to the floor. The body count is up, Gregory. And *you* are nearby every single time. You think that's a coincidence? Get in here, now!"

Before I have time to react, I'm knocked unconscious from behind.

Relectric to the floor. The body could it explored up... And you are ready, so is mine. You think that's a vein than we get in here, o see? beyond I saw time to start, I'm baffled untracks among it completind.

CHAPTER TWENTY-SEVEN
REVELATIONS

I wake in an unlit room. There's a slow drip, and someone else is breathing loudly, too.

How long have I been out?

Long enough for my neck to be sore. As my eyes adjust to the darkness, I speak softly, "I don't know where we are, or what they want. Are *you* okay?"

The voice replies at a matching volume, "Not sure. I've been in here so long, it's hard to say."

"You're still breathing, so that's a start, I suppose."

"They feed me once in the morning every day. And that's it."

The voice is familiar. I can't place it, though.

"I'm Greg," I whisper.

"I've been a prisoner for years," he says.

"What?"

"In a manner of speaking. Don't get angry with me."

"What?"

"Greg, it's Denny."

I'm in shock.

"I'm sorry, what?"

"Your brother, Denny."

I'm dumbfounded, moving toward the voice. "Denny's been dead for years."

"I had to be. This is the life I've chosen—to live in the shadows."

"Why?"

"He got me out. It took some phony records and whatnot, but he bought me out. Gave me a new life."

"What do you mean? Who?"

"John Fatts. He always had a vendetta about being shipped off to 'Nam. Shot himself in the knee to get out, broke into the document center, forged records, and got me 'dead.' I never wanted to be in the army, Gregory. That was all *you*. Dad practically forced my hand."

"Denny, I... I didn't know," I reply, slowly acknowledging and recognizing my long-lost brother's voice.

Denny nods. "That's not all, Gregory. Dad cheated... with Fatts' mother."

I shake my head. "No."

"It tore the family to shreds," he says. "I know you saw spats between mom and dad. Don't try to block it from your memory."

I shake my head, my emotions an escalating rollercoaster.

"You're saying you went along with this just to spite our parents' indiscretions?"

"I'm saying I'm antiwar. Dad was a fool. And he and Mrs. Fatts got caught. Anonymity's rarely overrated."

What does that mean? I'm livid. So shocked at this sick minute I could kill. I mean, literally kill.

Choke him to death and throw him in a swimming pool.

Hammer a cue ball into his thick skull fifty times over and watch him bleed.

I don't want to see him. Ever again. Not here. Not there. Not anywhere.

He's not here. This isn't happening. I'm just totally nuts.

I pull myself together, unable to stop shaking my head, my body trembling.

"You wanted to keep your miserable ass out of the war so bad you faked your own death?"

"I did what I had to, Gregory."

"No. You did what you wanted to. You lived for yourself! When you killed yourself, you killed her. Ruined us all!"

Denny shakes his head. "I've been around, brother. Watching you all from a distance, loving you in my own way, and hoping at some point we could finally intersect."

I grab him by the throat. The most physically disparaging thing I've ever done to anyone of my own volition. If I'm taking the bull by the horns, I might as well break them off.

"You're pathetic! Every man, woman, and child for himself, huh? All because you're some peace and love draft dodger?"

Denny shakes his head, breathless and out of words.

I let go. I guess there is some part of me that's still human, still compassionate. Nothing else shows it, though.

"What will dad say, asshole?" I fume, my teeth gritted. "It'll kill him. It will literally kill our old man. And that's all on you!" I say, shoving at him, tasting blood from biting my lip.

Denny's stunned by my physicality. He's flailing and floundering like some kind of limp fish. I was never one to do this when we were kids, I always looked out for him.

His disgusting grin tears me up inside, his sickening voice a path to further eruption. "Like momma always said, 'a good grudge gnaws right to the bone.'"

I envision her dead on the floor, her life over.

"Yeah. It's on your conscience. I can't believe this. And, all along, you were just down the street from us? That's kind of sick, man. No, it's really sick."

The light in the room comes on as a voice crackles through on an overhead intercom. "What's going on in there? Have you girls kissed and made up yet?"

I make eye contact with Denny for the first time in years.

My jets are cooling but the wrong move or set of words will push me right back over the edge with Denny's jugular ripped out and thrown in the floor.

I realize what it means to kill, what it takes to kill, and why a man can justify himself in the right moment. That floater in the swimming pool, he was never mine to kill. Some other man beat me to it, but any other night of the year, you put me and Denny out there, and that's him floating in the water.

I'm just stunned. I can't believe it's him — his hair combed, his face clean shaven, his waistline a sleek thirty-two.

I take a deep breath. "Denny, if you're a prisoner. Why do you look so... so well kept?"

"I've been on the television for years, Gregory. Have you just missed it? I almost thought when we shook hands that night that you knew. I convinced myself for a second it was your way of saying it was okay, that you forgave me."

Denny points to a wall. The blonde wig, the oversized teeth, the yellow jacket, and the sunglasses all hanging side-by-side on symmetrical hooks.

His voice becomes theatrical. "Play one... play all... play one... play all... Castle Productions Presents— *Twisted Hacks*... cable TV's bloodiest quiz show!"

I connect the dots. The reasons why. Odd jobs! That son of a bitch realtor, Lathrop, was the OIC that told us about Denny. All a damn charade. Just some stupid idiot hired to play an actor. He never went to Vietnam.

"Denny, why?"

"Vietnam broke me, my brother. Fatts built me into a better man, helped me to see everything about mom and dad that was so wrong. That's all any of us ever need. A little guidance, a little counsel from someone neutral to straighten our warped heads out."

He's still my kid brother. There's a million reasons to kill him, and a million more to love him, to nurture him, and to know him. That's how family operates, love 'em or hate 'em.

"You're brainwashed, Denny. We can get you some help."

Denny ignores the comment. "Let's go down the hall," he says, putting his arm over my shoulder. "There's something I'd like you to see."

My eyes adjust to the tunnel's lighting. I've got to see where this is going. If he's in the middle of all this and Fatts is part of it, there's hope that I'll find some kind of means to the madness. I'm led into another earthy board room of sorts with a long stone table. At the far side of the room, John Fatts waits for me, his face straight, his glare focused.

As we approach, he speaks first, "Preakle, there's an awful lot on my plate right now and I don't intend to waste more breath on you. I've got an enterprise to run."

"I don't follow."

I don't feel the anger for Fatts I should right now. He's tossed me around enough at this point with his actions at the school and beyond, and I'm just numb. I think I'm just so zapped by the shock of Denny. Thunderstruck is the only way I know to be, watching it all unfold like a jetlagged passenger.

"Greg, I've been juggling for years. The news people, the police, anyone else of consequence don't pay any mind because slug sucking's usually a private affair."

"How's that?" I ask. I genuinely wonder. I have no idea where he's going with this. If Fatts has been in on this long con, it chills me to the core to consider how long he's watched, spied, and manipulated my family. Whether passive or not, he's been there. I'm on the brink of dropping to the floor sick.

"You don't see any slug sucking bars... lounges... or stores around here, do you?"

His voice is so matter of fact, I could just gag.

"No."

"You don't see the kids in the alley behind the school doing a line of them, either, do you? Why is that?"

"I don't know."

This stupid line of questioning has me ready to throw punches again.

Fatts nods his head. "That's right! Because we keep the chirpers at bay. If someone's got too much to say, we deal with them in our own way..."

"What? I don't understand."

"I'm not here to monkey around with you, Preakle. Men get shattered kneecaps for less. You've seen *Goodfellas*, haven't you?"

Fatts stands up, moving into the light. He looks another pant size slimmer, his clothing notably baggier. "Walk over here with me."

He pulls back a door to a brightly illuminated room where harsh fluorescents light us up like corpses.

"Gregory, you have to see this," Denny says.

We go into the next room where there are a series of containers, vats, test tubes, and large tanks, the latter full of Tark slugs moving in a frenzy.

"We've been breeding 'em in here for a while now, Preakle," Fatts says. "It's lucrative, and we're about ready to go public."

"Go public? What the hell are you talking about?"

"Preakle, I had every intention of welcoming you into the fold, like my own brother, like *your* own brother. I've got no vendetta against you or Denny here. My qualm's with your pop. What he did to my mother. To my father."

"You've hurt us all," I remark. I'm nothing but a swirling mess.

Fatts sighs. "You know... I never meant for your mother to... 'off herself.' She was never part of the problem. She was just desperate for love and affection. Neglected for years by *your* sorry old man. Just a miserable old hag."

"Watch yourself!" I yell, cocking my fist back.

Denny puts his arm around me. "Mr. Fatts has a lot to offer, Greg."

"Why would you put up with this, Denny? This jerk off isn't worth it."

Fatts smiles, despite the comment. "Such a brilliant conclusion. Money talks, Preakle. It's a rule as old as time."

"What's your point?"

"It's simple," Fatts says. "Men are motivated by many things, but somewhere in our gut, we have that one thing that *really* drives us forward, and usually it's either power or money. And some of us strike it rich with both."

"I don't follow," I reply, looking at Denny. My brother's enamored with Fatts. There's no changing him.

I shake my head. "Denny, you can't keep going on like this. Let's get out of here. Fatts won't keep us against our will. Will you?"

Fatts flashes a grin. "I never have, and I never will. Loyalty comes naturally with me, Preakle. It always has. There's something endearing about a man with a southern charm. I've always ridden that wave, and it's panned out well for me. I've told Denny he could leave for years. And for some reason, the guy stays close to me. Like I'm some kind of blessing in his life—the father he never had."

"Let's go, Denny. There's another life ahead for us if you'll take it."

Denny sighs. "The money's too easy, Gregory. Isolation isn't such a bad thing. I walked out on my nation. *Twisted Hacks* keeps me vital, and a certain anonymity goes along with my character, too."

"You still want to be on that shitshow?"

"It's late-night entertainment, Gregory," Denny says. "There's a mystique to it, the special effects, the makeup, all of it."

Fatts motions me to move closer. "Not only that, Preakle, we regularly employ degenerates around town with the show. It's not like they were doing anything productive before but huddle the street corners and beg for a handout. We're giving them purpose *and* paying it forward at the same time."

I just want to storm out of the room. I've had enough.

"While you rake in the money from everything else... I know it was real, John! I know it, and you do, too. Are you seriously telling me no blood was spilled on the show?"

He scoffs. "Boy, TV's distorted your reality, son. Don't you think the cops and feds would be all over us if it was? You were just dizzy and spun out while you were there. Being disoriented has a tendency to make things look real when they're not. An anxious mind will do that, too. Go back and watch more of the footage and you'll see how cheesy the special effects look. Our memory can be a terribly unreliable narrator, the world's worst, in fact."

Denny nods, placing his hand on my shoulder. "He's right, Gregory. I swear. We have prosthetics. Most of the people that come on the show are missing an arm or a leg already. We just put a nice-looking one on before it airs, and then we tilt the cameras in such a way to give the appearance that the 'Final Verdict' is much worse than it is. Just camera trickery, tomfoolery really."

At some point, I realize any effort to reason or quibble with them is futile. I'm just going to let them finish up with what they want to say, and I'll be on my merry way.

"It's a real acid trip. Ha-ha!" Fatts says, opening the door. "Another thing, Preakle, I'm about to leave the school for good. I believe I've about worn out my welcome."

I rub the back of my neck. "If you had the means not to work in education, Mr. Fatts, why bother brushing elbows with working-class men and women? That seems like quite a charade to keep up. Too much unnecessary stress."

"Life's a game of chess, Preakle. Us elites are always prepping the board for our checkmate. Besides, teachers and school staff are ideal victims for the pyramid, Greg," he says.

"Pyramid? What are you talking about?"

"My patsies have been on the ground a while," Fatts says. "Most of them are long gone now. I've got to keep the Fatts machine well oiled. Castle Productions has always operated underground and with silent partners."

We walk through a dark passage, entering into another section of the tunnel. Denny motions me toward a chart staged in the corner where another primitive board room table sits, surrounded by disheveled chairs beneath more fluorescent lights. It's the same room attached to the school's basement.

I shake my head. "Why?"

"You see, Greg," Fatts says, "average working-class guys and gals are always looking for a side-gig to make some extra money—to afford a meal out, go to the movies, you know, that sort of thing. It's a calculated risk, but at least sixty percent of the time, I capitalize, and my organization does, too.

"I'm not sure I follow."

"It's the Tark slugs, Preakle," Fatts says, his voice electrifying "They go nuts over 'em. They get a few of their friends in on it, and we just keep reeling them in a few at a time. We just have to sink our hooks into 'em good and tight before we make a move. A slow burn, a long con, a leading conversation, a nice dinner out, and then... presentation night."

"You're kidding, right?"

Fatts shakes his head. "You're in luck, Preakle, we're doing one tonight."

CHAPTER TWENTY-EIGHT
PRESENTATION NIGHT

The presentation room is primitive, more like a cave than a traditional meeting space. As I look a little closer, I realize we're close to the basement of The Oak Hollow Hotel. I notice the backside of Jerry Greenwich's less than palatable aquamarine curtains and another access door that leads into the hotel. As of now, he seems like he's not part of the scheme, just a bystander, surely one that's well aware, but nonetheless not involved. Fatts and Denny lead me into the room.

"We'll get started in about fifteen minutes. There's someone else I'd like you to see." Fatts says. He moves across the room, knocking on another door marked PRODUCTION PLANT.

Dr. Hicks opens the door and enters the room in a lab coat.

"Dr. Hicks? What's going on here?" I ask, making eye contact with the former double duty shrink and physician.

Hicks moves to the center of the room and lifts at a panel revealing a chalkboard. "I take it he'll be staying for the presentation, then?" he asks Fatts.

Fatts nods. "Yeah. We've toyed with him long enough. It's about time to show him what's really happening around here."

"Toyed with me?"

I can't adequately express the rage. The fury. The hatred. I'm a man who appreciates justice. Somehow, these clowns are exactly the kind of guys that know how to walk the line, bending and skewing it whichever direction benefits them the most.

Before our conversation continues, attendees trickle into the room through Greenwich's office and out of the hotel basement. Some are familiar faces from the school, others are not. I notice the woman that cussed me at Castle Productions, concluding her to be Fatts' wife, Lynette. I don't think she saw enough of me or my arm to know it was me, so we're still in the clear.

Fatts stands at the podium as a room of about fifteen others huddle around the conference table.

A variety of presentation materials are handed out on print out sheets. Before I get to look them over closer, Fatts begins the lecture.

"Thank y'all for coming tonight. I know the locale here is a bit... underground, but so is your investment opportunity. Ha! We're not selling dome houses here. We're not asking for you to walk around and sell Amway. We're talking about real life, authentic people, and genuine relationships that are formed by a little creature God gave to us to enjoy. In the right hands, this thing can revolutionize science and medicine as we know it. On the handout, you'll find detailed schematics of our products in development, our sales results to date, and our plans for the future. But ultimately, we're offering you a simple path to a superhighway of monetary reward beyond your wildest dreams."

A man in a black coat speaks from across the room. "How can we know that this investment is going to yield long-term results?"

Fatts scoffs. "What kind of question is that? You've used the product, haven't you?"

"Well, yes, I have," he says.

"And you liked it, did you not?"

"Well, of course," the man replies, "but I can't do this recreationally forever. At some point, I'm a family man, a father, a husband, a businessman, a deacon. Eventually, I know the honeymoon has to end and you'll have me hooked on it, just like any other drug."

Fatts shakes his head and looks at Denny, who takes over. "No, sir, it's not like that at all. There's more to this than that. So much more. Certainly, the euphoric rush of a good slug suck is special, but as we've explored our boundaries with these peculiar critters, we've found all kinds of other uses, both holistic and medicinal."

"Such as what?" I ask.

"Folks," Fatts says, "Denny here has an appliance on his gut to keep him trim. You want to see? It's a prototype. I'm going to hand it over to our physician at large, Dr. Carl Hicks."

Hicks approaches the room's center and sketches on the chalkboard. He crudely draws two bodies side by side, one with a larger waist and another one smaller, marking them as A and B, respectively. "Yes, I've been conducting some experimental research for the enterprise for a while now... Looking at example A on the left, I want you to meet Denny, a thirty-eight-year-old male— a workaholic with no time for exercise and a 'six pack a night' beer habit... Now, let me ask you folks, how do you think he keeps up that perfect physique?"

The man in the black coat interjects, "Ex-Lax?"

"Hilarious. We have a comedian here tonight. Don't we, folks?" Dr. Hicks replies.

I shake my head, making eye contact with my brother. My attention's been so fixed on the front, I hadn't even noticed Dave sitting in the room amongst other attendees. Is *this* the meeting he was attending the other night? Man, am I gonna have words if it was.

"Example A, Denny, has an appliance installed... here," he says, drawing a small circular indentation near the lower stomach. "We essentially form a vacuum on the gut for the slug to extract the output before we move it into circulation. Now, you're in luck, because Denny is here tonight, and he's going to do a live demonstration. Denny, I want you to approach the scale across the room. Like every other night, we let Denny down a six-pack right before our presentation, so he's quite bloated from the excess alcohol. Step on the scale, please."

"189.3," Denny calls out.

"Not a bad weight for a six-footer, considering all the beer you just drank," Dr. Hicks says, "but before it can fully be absorbed, we're going to do what I call a 'system purge.' Denny's had a partial gastrectomy. Rather than bag the excess as is commonly accepted, we've routed a path for the discharge to excrete its own way, and allow a Tark slug to suck the output and share it while mating with other Tarks."

"This sounds disgusting," I call out.

"In principle, perhaps it does," Dr. Hicks says, "but the results are quick and fruitful. Please allow us to finish the demonstration before making any more comments."

"Fair enough," I mutter, making eye contact with my neighbor, Dave, who seems perplexed that I would heckle or challenge the doctor in front of the others.

"In experimental science, there are no absolutes— only open-minded Frankenstein's that aren't afraid to push the limits," Dr. Hicks says.

"Aren't you afraid of losing your license?" the man in the black coat asks.

Dr. Hicks shakes his head. "Ultimately, sir, the medical profession functions to help people survive, occasionally sustaining itself in the name of profitability with voluntary procedures. What I do behind closed doors doesn't have to be publicized and none of our investors are going to out those efforts. Are they?"

"But how can you make that foolproof?" the man interjects. "We don't want to be implicated in a conspiracy if something goes south here."

"We have our methods," Fatts replies, his teeth gritted. "Let Dr. Hicks continue the presentation, please. We'll answer further questions and comments at the close of the demo."

"Obviously, six stubbies and a soft pretzel are too much for one Tark, so we have a line of the slugs staged to address his intake," Dr. Hicks says. "In the center of the table, you'll see a bowl of additional Tarkies, so feel free to munch on one while we let the little critters work their magic on Denny. I assure you, there's no gimmick here. Pseudo-science, in the right hands, is still a science. Just ask your chiropractor about that. Proven results, time and time again."

I shake my head in a growing disgust as Denny raises his shirt and shows the attendees in the room a small tube just to the right of his bellybutton. As each participant examines it, he removes a gasket styled seal and stuffs the first slug into it.

"What's the risk here?" Dave asks. "I'm asking for a skeptical friend," he says, looking at me and smiling.

"It can't get into you if that's what you're asking," Dr. Hicks says. "It just sucks a portion of the nutrients out that your body deems nonessential. Once the slugs are good and full, we toss them back into the production plant for one more purification process."

"This whole thing is turning a little too wonky for me. I'd like to leave," the man in the black coat says.

"We never force our hand. The product sells itself to those worthy and never to anyone else," Fatts says. "I ask that you remain in your seat until the presentation ends. You might change your mind."

As Denny inserts a series of the Tarks, I note some of the droop to his trimming gut quickly disappearing.

"Thanks everyone for your patience," Dr. Hicks calls out. "Denny's on the final Tark now."

As he pulls out the slug, my brother smiles. "I think that's it," he says.

"Well, isn't that something?" Fatts says. "What did that take, about fifteen minutes?"

Dr. Hicks checks his watch. "Fifteen on the dot."

"You're going to find this hard to believe," Fatts says, "but fifteen minutes will completely reverse a bad bender and two bags of M&M's. Think of the potential here, folks!"

Dr. Hicks nods. "Denny, step on the scale, please."

Denny grins as he studies the scale and shows the room. "168.2"

"You've got to be joking?" I say, skeptically. "Twenty-one pounds in fifteen minutes?"

"You got it. Could make for a great commercial or tagline when we go public." Fatts says. He tightens up his belt buckle a notch and pull out a Tark from beneath his shirt as well. Moving toward the scale, Fatts says, "I'm in on it, too. I was 305 about an hour ago. With my added capacity, I've had a line of about thirty Tarks working on me. Any wagers?"

"Thirty," Dave says.

"Thirty-four," another man calls out.

"Zip," I mutter.

Dr. Hicks shakes his head. "Skepticism is natural, but belief unlocks new opportunity."

Fatts laughs as he steps on the scale. "Dr. Hicks channels his inner Confucius so he can write the little fortune cookie printouts and rake in some income on the side."

A few of the participants chuckle while I sit stone faced.

"And the verdict, Mr. Fatts?" Dr. Hicks asks.

"266.5 and three notches on the belt. Thirty-nine pounds in an hour, folks. Now, we don't want to doddle around too long here. The Tark slug empire is an emerging market, not for tightfisted conservatives that live in mommy's basement. We need some aggressive investors so we can take this thing public and accrue some real capital from the deal. What do you say?" Fatts says, his wide grin as glowing as I've ever seen it. "Your investment into the Tark enterprise is nine grand on the front end, but you're buying 'forever access' to our slug inventory, the marketing kit, and a ticket to many emerging medical advances."

Dave looks at me and smiles. "Go for it, buddy. I'm *already* invested!"

"Na," I reply.

The man in the black coat speaks up, placing the handouts on the table. "Not for me. I wish you all well, though. This is just too weird."

I sit there in silence as several others raise their hands, buying into the sales pitch like kids in a candy store. Rather than say anything else, I sit back, knowing my indecision will come at a cost. As others stand up, chat about the product, sign paperwork, and are immediately coerced, my knees buckle beneath me.

***

I awake with Denny, Dr. Hicks, and a few others hovering above— brown goo seeping from their pores slowly, their beady little eyes, more resemblant of bugs than people.

Denny's voice is distorted or my ears are underwater. The room's shaking, its colors brighter than I'd hope them to be. "Are you okay, brother? Is your blood sugar low or something?"

I bite my lip and shake my head, motioning to the others to give me some space. As I sit up on the floor, I struggle to find the words.

"What's the matter, Preakle?" Fatts calls out. "Cat got your tongue?"

I swear, if these goons drugged me... slugged me. Whatever we're going to call it... Something's lodged in the back of my throat. I try to hook it out with my index finger. I gag up a slew of brown goo and a Tark slug drops to the ground.

"What the hell is going on?" I yell. "I didn't take one. Who did this?"

The others surround me and begin chattering in an eerie unison. Whatever effect the slug consumption had on me throws me off kilter as the walls of the room sway side to side and the fluorescent lights dance with rainbows.

"It's okay to crack, Preakle," Fatts says. "I've said it before. I'll say it again. Life's too short to keep a stick up your ass. We just thought we'd speed things along after you passed out."

"You had no right," I say, my voice growing stronger. "This is *my* choice."

"We have every right. That's your signature on the paperwork right there. Is it not?"

I study the sheet. It's clear I've been taken advantage of, but there's no way out. "You sons of bitches! You got me high on slugs to con me out of $9,000?"

"No, Preakle. You signed the paperwork in the Castle Productions studio when you went on the show. It's all a package deal, under the table handshakes and whatnot. I guess you just missed some of the fine print in your desperation," Fatts says, grinning. "I know you helped yourself to one at the school, anyhow, did you not? Will Hoblitz always kept an inventory. And the crazy codger seemed to have done it right before I blew his ass up with the water heater gag. He was sloppy and senile, Greg. I kept catching him with Tark slugs in his shirt pockets, trying to slip 'em in the kids' lunchboxes, taking advantage of my teachers. I couldn't be having that. I won't have any predators in my school!"

I shake my head, my senses and wits coming back to me in waves. "What about Coach Simmons? Did you have something to do with that?"

"You think I'm just going to spill my guts and confess to everything in one sitting?" Fatts asks, laughing and looking toward Denny.

"It can't hurt to ask, can it?"

"It can hurt," he says, clutching my nub and squeezing it beneath his arm.

"What are you, a fourth grader? Where's your common sense?" I ask.

"I left it at the door, Preakle. I'm a disturbed man, with a craving to settle old scores and make a little money along the way."

"Denny, let's get out of here," I say, pulling away from Fatts.

"Gregory, we've already been over this. Fatts is a better man than you're giving him credit for."

"Mom's dead, Denny. She's dead because of you and this man, what he did to you."

"No," Fatts says. "She's dead because Dr. Hicks swapped her pills out. Cranked up the prescription a couple of notches, and gave her a new set of voices to listen to in that wild head of hers. The medicine can be dangerous, Greg."

"What? What medicine?"

Dr. Hicks nods. "As much as I don't want to admit it, Greg, we switched your mother from her normal antidepressants to a more holistic approach."

"What are you talking about?"

"A few years ago, we developed a new line of the Tark slugs in pill form. We take an excretion from the little guys' innards, crush it up, dry it out, and pop it into a pill. It cures just about everything and makes the stress melt right away," he says, a gulp engulfing his throat.

"But?"

Dr. Hicks sighs. "But they're highly addictive and when overprescribed, they can get out of control."

"You're saying my mother got addicted to experimental slug pills?"

"She signed off and consented to the study, Greg. That's all that's needed until someone else takes out a POA or she's fully committed to our care."

"Why does it feel like you're all characters in a bad dream? This is wearing me out," I say, my voice escalating.

"It's a side-effect of the slugs, Greg," Dr. Hicks answers. "They can... make you paranoid. Sometimes, they make your memories take over your dreams. Fatts gave you some of the high-pH slugs to 'catch you up' with the rest of our participants. I guess it was just a little more than you could handle."

"What?"

"It's not a well-known fact yet," Dr. Hicks says, "but Tark slugs distort your dreams and realities, throwing off your ability to make rational decisions much like other hallucinogens often can. It's not every time, and it's not all the time. Usually, it just amplifies things a little. When you get down to brass tax, people hate reality. And, I'd venture to say, adding some texture and color to life is exactly what they need to sustain them. If the number one cause of murder and suicide is nervous breakdown, then it only stands to reason that sucking a slug now and then may be 'just what the doctor ordered.'"

"Your center of gravity, your sanity, it's all thrown off," I say. "Do you think people would willfully allow that if they realized how disruptive it could be to the norm... to their equilibrium?"

"Probably not," Dr. Hicks replies, "but we're trying to run a business here. To be profitable."

Fatts pats Denny on the back. "Tell him, Denny."

"I've been liquored up for years. Until John got me switched to Tarks and gave me purpose. My mind's been to hell and back in every way you could imagine. I've found my inner peace now, though."

I scoff, an uncommon anger spiking to an all-time high. "Mom's dead. Dad cheated. You host a trash TV show better suited for the sludge pile? How can you be at peace? What about all the years in between? Where the hell have you been?"

"I've been finding myself, Gregory."

"When did *Twisted Hacks* come on... '87? What about all the time before that? You just hid out the entire time?"

"Everybody cheats a little, Greg. It's a matter of who gets caught along the way," Denny says. "I've watched you for years. Your dull, monotonous life, a depressing existence. And that's why we did all this..."

"Did what?"

"It's about time we come clean with you, Preakle," Fatts says. "Dave's been swapping the beers from your fridge the last couple of weeks with a Tark-infused beer to loosen you up and widen your horizons. We wanted to give your life the change it needed. To transform you."

"What?"

Fatts cracks the top of another beer open and continues, "Life gets a little boring, doesn't it? We beg for a break from the monotony, to numb the pain of the past, most of us growing to prefer distorted realities. All those bodies you saw, the mysterious deaths, their appearing connected. Well, they are. They're all connected to you, Preakle!"

"No! No! No! I didn't kill anybody!" I yell, my voice echoing down the long corridor. "Don't pin this on me."

"I never said *you* killed anyone," Fatts says, a subtle grin forming at the corners of his mouth.

"And neither did we," Denny says. "We've been messing with you."

The blood inside me boils. "What the hell are you saying?"

"Greg, I produce low budget cable shows that glorify blood and guts," Fatts says. "You don't think I could stage a few deaths to screw with you? I got a little creative, hired a few police officers to moonlight, and brought in a couple of actors to keep things interesting. Hell, my wife and I own a dad-gum TV station. Here lately we throw in some faux news reports, get your neighbors to play along, and you all the sudden accept it all as gospel? Change the station in your life, now and then, Preakle. Wake up and smell the coffee! If Channel 33 can run shows like

Twisted Hacks and *Freaky Fred,* of course, they'll play along with a few fake deaths. It's about that time of the year, anyhow. Find some Halloween spirit and loosen your tight ass up!"

"What are you saying?" I ask. My heart pounding harder by the minute, my fury intensifying. "You staged these deaths and put me through this just for your own twisted amusement... all for the hell of it? You shut down an entire school? Wasted police resources? Ran fake news reports?"

Fatts laughs. "No, Greg. The school was always open. We just ran you away from it and said we were closing to keep stringing you along. That's why we did it after hours. Maybe Denny and I sucked one slug too many when we concocted the plan. It was your hazing ritual, Preakle. The gateway to your new career. Everyone else played along because I paid 'em to," Fatts says, moving closer, resting his hand on my shoulder. "I told you that day on my boat that the job would transform you. I hope I delivered on my promise. That's all we were hoping for."

Denny nods and says, "Yeah. Twenty years working at the same swimming pool and not a single redeeming moment in your life—same old, same old, just skimming by, paycheck to paycheck. Can't you make more out of it? I have to live vicariously through you, Gregory."

I roll my eyes at Denny. "You're the last person to say anything about making more out of my life. You're a hermit!"

"You're right," Denny says. "I'm also well-compensated."

Fatts chuckles. "You passed the test, Preakle. And just on the other side of that door, Pool Man, sits a table full of the smiling faces of coworkers and acquaintances you thought were dead. Do yourself a favor now and then and get out of that head. Suck a slug. Enjoy life. And know that tomorrow may still be your last."

CHAPTER TWENTY-NINE
LAUGHING BEHIND CLOSED DOORS

I sit at a table across from Coach Simmons, Dave, AP Robbins, and Will Hoblitz, among a few other familiar faces, as we share slices of pepperoni pizza. They're all laughing and having a good time. I'm a wet blanket. I mean, who wouldn't be? After all the shit they put me through, all the turmoil, the strife, the blood, the guts, the sleepless nights. Maybe it just hasn't sunk in long enough, and I'm a little too tolerant. Something tells me I'll just resent it more with time. I don't know, though. My skin's gotten thicker and I'm a hell of a lot more calloused, so I guess I don't care. Sheesh. I really am the next Will Hoblitz.

Detective Penske, so I'm told, is working the graveyard shift at the station and unable to join us. The bullet in the head gag having been described as a work of special effects and trick lighting. Denny sits next to me, his arm around me as we all suck back a round of beers in an undefined meeting space near the school basement. I'd rather not be this chummy, but the haze from the Tarks seems to keep me more agreeable than I should be. I feel stuck in a dream in this moment, but every time I pinch myself, I realize it's not.

After I finish my pizza, I join in on the conversation. "The makeup, the effects— all of it was done so well. I mean, Simmons, were you actually jammed on the rim? How did you keep a straight face for all that time?"

"It's all effects, Greg. They took a mold of my face and body and went to town with it. You just didn't get close enough to realize it was fake."

Fatts walks by, briefly adding to the discussion. "You have a combination of the special effects crew from *Twisted Hacks* and *Freaky Fred* to thank for that and our new network, The Nightmare Channel. We're going national next season!

They had a crew in town finalizing the terms of our deal and I told 'em I wanted to demo a few scenes at the school for a movie I was making. I left you a damn tape to watch. Did you ever find it?"

I nod. "Yeah. The editing was choppy, but seriously, the blood, the smells, the looks, all a little too good," I reply.

"So, yeah," Denny says, pulling out a megaphone from beneath the table and speaking into it a second. "This beer's got a Tark infusion in it, too. Thankfully, it's odorless. All the benefits of a 'suck and go' with no aftertaste. The best part is that it keeps things lighter, makes people a little smarter, and more self-aware, but otherwise, it's just a good old-fashioned brew like everyone's grandpa used to drink."

"You were the one taunting me in the school, Denny? I thought you had to stay hidden under your rock."

"Yeah. I have my methods to get out and around town. It's a lot of wigs, sunglasses, fake beards, that kind of stuff. You get used to the charade after a while. I slipped in through the basement a few times. I just had to wait until Fatts gave me the go ahead."

"You have some nerve, man."

Simmons leans in toward me, his beer breath more than I can stomach. "Greg, I hear the Spartans won a game while I was 'dead.' I guess I have *you* to thank for that."

"Well, the difference between a bad coach and a good one is... a better team," I say, grinning in relief that the less than likeable coach is still alive and kicking.

"I'm leaving the education profession, anyway," he says.

"Why's that?"

He nods. "I've been promoted to a 'distributor' role."

My heart skips a beat as I struggle to process. "What?"

"You mean, no one's explained the phases to you?" Simmons asks.

"Distributor?" I ask, perplexed by the word choice. "What do you mean, *phases*?"

"The structure's formalized now, Greg," Simmons replies. "When we take this national and go public, this whole thing will catch on quickly. We're not just giving out slugs to random people on street corners anymore. This is all a strategic and tactical business model. A lot of it's simply reading body language in a chat to figure out if the person is worth the time."

"Worth the time to what?" I ask.

"To, you know, lead them to the next step of the pyramid. First, we start our clients on the slugs as a 'consumer.' After a few weeks of selling them on proven results, you know... the euphoria, the lower stress, the reduced anxiety, the option for the weight loss add-on, and so on, we're less than subtly adding a growing dependence on the product and moving them into a 'seller' role —you know, internal access to discounts for family members and to a select few close friends. It's not a cheap buy in, though, as you've heard. The upfront cost helps the distributors stay afloat and compensates the existing sellers. Once we recruit enough to go under us, that's when we get promoted into the 'distributor' role, and the money really starts pouring in. The trouble is, if our consumers and sellers can't meet quota, we're all put in a difficult position to fund the enterprise."

"What happens if they can't meet quota?" I ask.

Simmons shakes his head. "Don't know. I just keep my guys motivated. I live and die by the same motto. 'The fewer questions asked, the better the results.'"

"AP Robbins, I thought that coffee was the end of the line for you."

"Someone's got to teach you how to check a pulse, Greg. You're a little too gullible," she says. "By the way, my name's Julia Wells, paid actress."

"Are you kidding?"

She smiles at me. "Nope! I played the part pretty well, didn't I?"

"What about the ambulances... the police... the other teachers... the way they all went along with it?"

"Preakle, when you own a town the way I do, you can get away with just about anything," Fatts says, coming back from the next room and plopping a metal bucket of slugs on the table to go along with the pizza. "A line of slugs... on the house," he says. "It pays to have connections. I call in a few favors, and we make things happen."

The group takes the slugs in succession. I'm not up for anymore.

Will Hoblitz nods, cracking a huge grin. "We're taking the product to California."

I study the old timer closer. "You're what?"

"We're taking it to California," he says. "I thought the water heater incident was a great way to scare you shitless. You came in with an attitude that needed adjusting, and here we are now. You're adjusted. Fatts changed my life with the Tarks. I want to spend my twilight years doing something I enjoy, not mopping some damn kid's vomit every day."

"Are we going to have to force your hand, Preakle?" Fatts asks. "You loosened up a lot the last time we strung you out on the slugs."

"No. I'm not feeling it right now," I reply.

"As for California," Fatts says, "this whole thing will catch on better out in LA. We can infuse slugs into everything and sell, sell, sell. The euphoria alone is enough to get most people into it. And it's all completely legal! It'll trickle its way into Hollywood, advertisements, and before you know it, we'll sell a shmuck like Kevorkian on it and get him to plug it all over national TV shamelessly."

"Sounds like a plan to me," Denny says.

An overwhelming anxiety overtakes me. They're all in on it. They're all making money from it. And I'm sitting here the village idiot, along for the ride again. It's not entirely my fault. I mean, if the Tark slugs are making me a little too "go with the flow," what else is a man to do?

Fatts grins. "It's all a bit much to swallow in one sitting. Isn't it, Preakle? Never thought your weird boss could get weirder, did ya? Ha-ha!" he says, slapping me on the back.

"We're sitting on stacks of cash, Greg. Tens of thousands," Denny says.

I nod. "So, do you think you actually have the capacity to mass produce these things? Aren't you at the mercy of nature here?"

Fatts agrees. "We were for a while, but as we've grown out the production plant and figured out the best ways to supercharge these guys, we're finding new paths to watch them 'be fruitful and multiply.'"

"Don't you have a way with words?" I reply, rolling my eyes.

"I'll let you in on a little secret, Preakle. The fat suckers are more potent. They twist up their hermaphroditic bodies in a little corner and get busy. They can pop out fifteen, twenty slugs at a time if we're lucky, sometimes more. You do the math. Get a few hundred moving at once, and the next thing you know, you're looking at tens of thousands of 'em."

"So, you're saying the demand hasn't caught up with the supply?" I ask, stroking my cheeks.

"Not yet."

"What's the shelf life, then?"

"They don't lose their potency. The rush supercharges with age like a fine wine," Fatts says. "That's part of why we're moving to LA. Those people are so fixated on hip trends and looking good, I have no doubt it will take off. Lipsticks, implants, hair regrowth, the list goes on and on."

"The discharge of these little slugs has *that* many applications?"

Fatts nods. "It's just the tip of the iceberg."

"So, why am I here?"

Fatts picks up another slug and sucks it. He sits down a moment, taking some time to react. "I need someone to be my poster child for the product. I was hoping *you* might do the honors?"

"Why me?"

"Because Preakle, statistics show that 37% of people are more likely to believe the words of a cripple or a handicap. We'll give you a script, you'll do a commercial, and we'll pay you well at our public product launch." Fatts grins as he stands back up. "Don't worry, Preakle, we'll have people flocking to the product like it's the gosh darn cure to everything. What do you say about that? A six-figure income, an arm full of beautiful Los Angeles women, a fresh start. It's all yours, a big happy ending for all of us."

"Can't you just fake a cripple or handicap like everything else? Clearly you have the means," I say, my sarcasm apparent.

"Of course we could. But why would we, when we have the real deal an arm's length away? Ha! It would keep you and Denny together."

The man's wildly delusional, but he's got such an influence on the rest. There's no point in belaboring the point because they're all right with him in a bizarre lockstep. I find my words.

"I'm not sure I want to be in the public eye. I prefer my quiet, simple life," I reply.

"What if I could promise you more, Preakle?" Fatts asks, his demeanor changing.

"It's not a matter of money, John. It's the principle of the thing."

"Walk with me," Fatts says. We go around mounds of slugs feeding one after another, sticky and slimy. His own neck dropping gobs of brown goo to the floor.

I shake my head, moving toward the door. "These slugs have ruined you, but I won't let them ruin me."

Denny grabs me by the arm, yanking me toward him. "Join the movement. Come with us to California, Gregory. Get a fresh start. You deserve it," Denny says.

I sigh. "Guys, I'm not here to stop you. I just want to appreciate my own life a little more and pay that positivity forward to other people. I've been too apathetic for too long."

Fatts purses his lips and nods. "Alright, Preakle. I've got the message. The jig's up, Denny. Let him go."

I approach Denny, shaking hands with and embracing him. "Dad's dead to me," he says, "and I'm dead to him, and we're both better off that way."

"I'm not here to tell you how to run your life," I say. "That's between the two of you. We may not always see eye to eye, but one thing will never change. I love you, brother."

"I love you, too, Gregory. Take care of yourself," he says as we embrace. "Godspeed."

CHAPTER THIRTY
HARD TRUTH

My trek across town feels unscripted. I'm lonely. I want to talk to dad. I'm a little shocked I didn't get offed by Fatts or the rest. I'm just the butt of some stoner's joke. I don't know if to feel embarrassed, emasculated, or emancipated. Maybe I'm all three, but I'll never tell.

They say in crime, motive means everything, but sometimes, I wonder if that's only part of it. The other driving force, too much free time, or just a way to break up monotony. Why is it, then, that career criminals are not all poor men just scrounging for their next meal or working to provide for their families? Rich men often share the same vice, and then, for the rest of us somewhere in the middle, we go home at night, turn on the news, and hear their stories, over and over, and thanking God the little switch in our own head didn't flip to something crazy.

As I pull in to dad's property, it's vacant and dilapidated, a rapid decline from my last visit. The grass is overgrown, weeds are popping up all over the place, and the picket fence is falling over. Something's gone terribly wrong. Dad's too much a perfectionist to allow this place to fall apart so quickly.

I've already decided I'm not here to disrupt life or to snitch on Denny. I don't think I'm even here to lecture him on getting busy with another woman. This conversation is between the two of us, and us alone.

I don't reach for the hide-a-key this time. Getting up to the house, I knock on the door several times. There's no answer. I call out to dad, peering into the windows that are on either side of the door.

"Dad? It's Greg."

My pop stumbles toward the door. He pulls it open and lets me in, reeking of booze.

"What are *you* here for?" he asks, less than cordially, a hint of slur in his voice.

"I just wanted to stop by and see how you were. Are you feeling alright? Things are looking a little worse for wear around here, dad."

Dad sighs for an extended second. "I've been better. I guess this is just part of getting older."

"What do you mean? You seemed fine the other day."

He invites me in, and we sit down on the sofa. "Well, the truth is, Greg, I'm overwhelmed."

"By what?" I ask.

"By guilt."

"Why?"

His words come out slowly. "I killed a man, and I'm having trouble forgiving myself."

"The man in Korea? Dad, it's been almost forty years. You're beyond the statute of limitations on that, aren't you? You have to move on at some point."

His face is colorless, his bloodshot eyes and body, so much weaker than they used to be. "I distracted myself from it as long as I could, Greg."

I nod him along. "Go on, then. I'm no priest, but if you need to confess something, I've got time."

"Greg, I owe apologies to people I can't give them to— for foolish things I did a lot of years ago," he says, a tear going down his cheek.

I follow suit, struggling to find words. "I know you cheated, dad. What's in the past is in the past. Let's start over— while we still have each other."

"Greg, that's not it."

"Okay, so, what is it, then?"

"I lied to you, son."

"Lied? About what?"

"Everything."

"Dad? What are you saying?"

"I don't have a police scanner, Greg. I killed him."

"You what?"

"It was me. Suffocated the jerk and threw him in. The cops haven't come looking and probably never will, but I can't carry this guilt to the grave."

"You're kidding."

Dad looks all but gone as he speaks, the affectation in his voice completely flat, "When I look in the mirror each morning, I see a killer, cold and calculated on a whim, snapping in the heat of the moment. Law enforcement and military men can see it, too. I can't go out anymore, Greg. I can't be seen. It's got to end for me, son."

I'm frustrated, but nowhere near as much as I am with Denny. Dad's a grieving widower and a recovering divorcee who's "lost a son" and deals with the trauma of a helicopter crash in Korea. Still, there's a part of me that has to challenge him here. He deserves to be poked, maybe even prodded.

"Dad, you knew I'd worked that pool for years. You told me yourself, you were sick of me doing the same job for so long. That pool was my life, dad. You had no right."

"You're right, but Greg, I've sat on the board of investors for The Oak Hollow Hotel all throughout the renovations. I just never had the heart to tell you. Some nights, me and a few of the others would huddle out back behind the hotel after our meetings just to soak in the evening air. I'd watch you work, admire you. You're my son, after all."

"You guys would loiter behind that storage building? You're one of the brainiacs that covered my pool with a blacktop? Come on, dad."

"Yeah, we'd wrap up our meetings, stand around a while, and shoot the shit a few minutes. The weather's just been too damn good not to enjoy a cigar under the stars."

"How come you never said hi?"

"I didn't want you to think I somehow had influence over your employment. A man shouldn't be robbed of his dignity on account of his parents. It's *your* livelihood, not mine."

"I heard this man... the man you killed was an out of towner. Who? Why?"

He shakes his head. "Larry Fatts lived in Barton Hills. He's been a headache as long as I've sat on the board. I guess you know his son, the Principal."

"You killed Larry Fatts? How did this miss the newspapers? I thought this guy was as good as a John Doe around here."

"Larry had a beef with that editor over there at the Statesman. I forget his name, Dorse. Yeah, Hal Dorse. Dorse is an investor, too. Dorse froze out the media coverage and we all just agreed to move Larry out of the way."

"So, what you're really admitting to me, dad, is that the entire board of investors at the hotel killed him. It's not all yours to shoulder. Just because you were the hands that did the deed, the entire group's to blame."

Dad nods, a relief showing on his face. "I guess you're right. I've been looking at this all wrong."

"Did Jerry have anything to do with it?"

"No. Jerry was asked to leave early that night," Dad says. "We didn't see eye to eye about the pool... or the blacktop. We were all drunk and flustered after the board meeting that night, and I got a little loose lipped and mouthed off. When he found out I got busy with his old lady all these years later, he punched me, and I just lost it. A few minutes later, I had a plastic sack over his head, stealing his last breaths. The pool was just a convenient drop zone. You know, Greg, I've given the façade that I've lived for my nation all these years, but I've always lived for myself. And I've got hell to pay for that."

I sigh, teetering on the brink of breakdown. "You know what you have to do, dad. I'm not here to play God. I've got to go." I shake his hand; his grip's clammy and weak. We embrace without words, and I walk out the door.

My drive down his unkempt driveway feels forever long. I know the old man's eaten up with guilt and remorse, but I carry an unexplained peace, knowing that despite mistakes and killing a man, owning it really is half the battle. Dad may have burned every bridge for redemption left, but he'll rest a lot easier owning his failures.

CHAPTER THIRTY-ONE
NEW BEGINNINGS

1992

I arrive home at Cove Ridge after another good day at the school. I'm on day shift now one hundred percent of the time and our new principal is just lovely. It turns out Principal Robbins was such a hit around the school in her short tenure that Julia Wells was named the new lady in charge. She's got an MFA, and our district's loose enough to let that slide. I was shocked when I found out she liked hair metal. I felt betrayed at first, knowing she tore my posters down despite loving the bands. Now, *that* was method acting right there. I'm spicing things up at home, too. I haven't slept in the recliner in weeks. I've taken Julia out a couple of times for dinner and drinks, too. Ever since my awakening, my new beginning, last fall, whatever the hell that crazy ride was with Fatts and company, I have to admit, I've found a new happiness. So, I guess I owe them a little something. Twisted as it all was, it changed me.

Something's different around here.

The air's cleaner, the trailers all shine and sparkle a little brighter, and suddenly crazy cat ladies like Joan seem less annoying than they used to.

Dave's packing up the back of a U-Haul, collecting the last of his beer garden collages. Otherwise, the truck looks full of his taxidermy.

"Well, good gracious, neighbor," I call out. "This is the cleanest I've seen your place in ages. Are you leaving or what?"

"No. I just have a moving truck outside for my personal pleasure," he says. "Of course I'm leaving. I'm going to California. It'll be a good fresh start."

"So, you're really into this whole move to California bit, too? I never took you for a nine-to-five sort of career man. Don't you think that's what this will translate to long term?"

"Well, maybe," he says.

"A corporate office isn't going to run itself," I say. "And I'm assuming that's where Fatts wants most of you."

He nods. "Well, I figure if I'm gonna ride into the sunset, I might as well do it in 'the Sunshine State.'"

"You mean... 'the Golden State.'"

He scoffs. "Yeah, whatever. Sunshine state... golden state, close enough."

"This doesn't seem just a little too good to be true to you?" I ask.

"Nope. I'm on the Tarkano payroll now, and it's only taken about three checks to have enough to buy out this entire trailer park."

"Tarkano?"

"Yeah," he says, "the new name for our enterprise, Tarkano."

A list of sarcastic replies runs through my head, but I decide to keep them to myself. "Why not buy out Cove Ridge, then? Owning a trailer park seems more up your alley."

"I'll try not to take that personally," he says, pulling the rear door to the U-Haul down.

"Keep in touch. Don't become a statistic out there. I hear LA's murder capital USA."

"Oh, I don't know. I'm not too worried. The other guys have already had a few months to settle out there and seem to be enjoying it just fine. I take my life one day at a time, and I like it better that way, and uh, I owe you an apology, neighbor."

"Why are you just now telling me? We've had beers on the patio for weeks since this all came to light."

"I didn't want you to flip out on me, man."

"So, what is it, then?"

"Those harassers bothering you here at the house, they weren't any of Fatts' thugs. They were mine. I was short the nine grand to invest in Tarkano and you were just the perfect low hanging fruit. Please don't take it personally. With royalties in now, you'll find all of it paid back in a briefcase. I dropped it off in your living room."

I shake my head. "Dave, I don't know what to say. Those guys had guns. You shot out their window! That was one elaborate ruse."

He nods. "I guess what I'm trying to say is, don't worry about replacing those nine-millimeter shells or that six-pack we talked about."

"You're telling me all the shenanigans over here at Cove Ridge, were you... and not Fatts?"

"Guilty as sin," he says, a smirk coming across his face.

"You put me through all that to pay your way into a pyramid scheme? You're one hell of a neighbor," I say, struggling not to smile, considering the unforeseen outcome.

"Well, I think I told you before, my creativity can get a little stale. Still friends, neighbor?"

"Since you paid it back and owned up, I guess. Good luck in California. Don't go growing some long ponytail, though. That might change things between us. You need help packing anything else up?"

"Nope," he says, climbing into the cab of the U-Haul, and checking his watch. "I'm out of here."

"See you later."

As sunset arrives, I wave at him. I walk back across to my porch, making eye contact with Joan. She's out chain smoking again, her oversized Siamese cat resting in her lap. I wave. She returns a wave and turns around. A few minutes later, she comes out and tosses me a bag of cheesy snacks.

"From Finland," she says.

"Thanks!" I call out.

She waves and goes back inside.

Stolz comes across the lot in his wife beater and baggy blue jeans, immediately putting a FOR RENT sign on the door of Dave's former residence.

"You don't waste any time, do you?" I ask.

He shakes his head. "I'm running a business here. Every hour this place is vacant, I'm losing money."

"Take care," I say, paying up next month's rent early.

"Thanks. I'm glad to see you're on your feet," he says, walking away and back to his house.

Coming into the house, there's a note stuck to the front door and a new Flitz stubby bottle wind chime hanging up.

> *Greg, I'm sorry for the inconvenience. Just inside, you'll find*
> *a briefcase with $9,000 and your voided contract.*
> *– Dave Levett, Distributor*
> *Tarkano Enterprises*

I don't bother counting the cash. I know it's all there. I grab a cold one, slug infused or not, I guess I don't really care. Plopping into my recliner, I turn on the television. It's on a commercial break.

The familiar voice of John Fatts is dubbed over a series of peaceful images of streams, mountains, and beaches. There's a clanking of wine glasses and people laughing in a restaurant before the final cut to a group playing water volleyball in a swimming pool. A zooming camera shot moves toward a pair of slugs sliding on the ground slowly side by side.

"Slug sucking gets a bad rap. There are mountains of potential here. It's not just a drug. It's a revolutionary way to improve your life naturally, superseding anything you've ever seen before. Invest now to change! Don't let *your* life end in misery. Cure your ailments! This message was brought to you by Tarkano Enterprises, a new lifestyle revolution."

Denny comes on the screen shirtless, his body toned and drenched in bronzer, his voice more masculine than it actually is. He sits on a beach with beautiful women in swimsuits lounging on either side of him. "I tried Tarkano for a few weeks and the wildest of *my* dreams came true. Make yours do the same today by calling toll free, 1-800-TARKANO. Again, that number is 1-800-Tarkano. 827-5266. Operators are standing by, and supplies are limited. Don't miss your chance. I didn't," he says. He drops in the dirt as one woman leans in and kisses him. The camera narrows in closer to her back. A drop of brown goo hits the sand just beneath as the commercial ends.

Immediately after, familiar music cues and I see Denny come on the screen, his blonde wig, and sunglasses, bigger, better, and brighter. "Play one... play all...

play one... play all... Castle Productions Presents— *Twisted Hacks*... cable TV's bloodiest quiz show! Join us tonight for a wild and bloody ride!"

"Fatts is right. Life *is* too short..." I say, throwing the remote at the TV. When euphoria leaves the lights on even one second too long, the best thing we can do is turn them off.

THE END

AUTHOR'S NOTE

This story's peculiar origins were likely influenced by things like *Cocoon*, 80s slashers, hair metal, Chuck Palaniuk, Stephen King, Kurt Vonnegut, David Cronenberg, my odd fixation with the failed 3DO gaming system, summer swim lessons with my daughter, Alice, and the birth of my son, Andrew, whose middle of the night feedings left my mind racing on tangents at obscure hours and me wide awake in the wee morning hours as he kicked his feet across my keyboard in beautiful rhythms.

***

I don't think I ever got along well with kids, even as a kid, really. I mean, I had friends, and I had acquaintances. Thankfully, I was never much the trouble causing type.

Or was I?

Maybe my memory's failing me like it does most of us when we prop up the better, happier moments of our past. Most people look back and quickly gloss over their weaknesses, taking a heck of a lot more time to highlight their strengths. We're educated that way in college to prep us for job interviews—but reviewing those things isn't nearly as interesting. Allow me to demonstrate.

I realize the "squeaky clean" kid I thought I was may have only been a figment of my imagination— at least for one summer, when a newly made acquaintance contributed to more harm than good as an influence. I remember the two of us hopping a fence in the neighborhood pool, destroying the HOA clock, pitching it into the water and laughing before a gigantic cloud of guilt could hover just above us. Later that day, before our petty crimes were discovered, we tagged the side of my folks' pink-bricked mailbox with a can of leftover spray paint my mom used to get my sister's ballet shoes the correct color (Bear in mind, these were the days before this kind of purchase was a click away, and money was a little tight.).

And why did I do this?

Peer pressure from another kid, that's all it was. It's the pack mentality. It leads us to do things we'd never dare to do on our own! I don't think the other kid would've either. Typical "pissantics."

Among other items from the highlight reel that summer, I peed in a Duplo bucket at a friend's house, told a neighborhood kid their mom drank too much beer, and turned one of our living rooms into a graveyard using baby powder as the white dust covered our blue carpet. *May God bless my mother, and every other mother out there, too.*

It didn't stop there; I even remember squirting caulk on a freshly poured slab of a brand-new home in our suburban neighborhood (Those poor people probably still have an indentation under their carpet. I'll be mailing them a check before this is published...) Crazy thing is, these unjailed escapades were all in one summer, more or less, and I was only eight years old. I spent a lot of days in "time out" for shenanigans like that, and I certainly deserved it.

Back to kids— my getting along with them doesn't mean I didn't love or relate to them, then or now. I just have to work a little harder to connect as I shoulder everyday burdens and juggle responsibilities on a given day.

To be honest, I get tired of horror stories that revolve around a bunch of high school students committing the seven deadly sins and getting slashed by a masked psycho, so I thought I'd incorporate some elements of the classic slasher films of the 80s and 90s but add my own preferred flavor of adults to change things up a little.

Brevity is something in a book that can either make it work well or totally kill it. For the sake of this work, I've tasked myself with conciseness. It's also a step into the first person POV, which I find limiting but also more emotionally connecting for my audience. Love a character. Hate a character. Do what you want with them. At the end of the day, it's all in the spirit of fun.

As for writing *this* book, a man can only muse for so long before he ventures off into uncharted territories and loses himself in a sea of crashing waves, tall tales, and manic bursts of laughter and screams best described as emotional overloads. It makes for a whale of a ride, but if we spend too much time in any one given place, we start to live there in our mind in perpetuity. And that's what most storytellers do. When we're overwhelmed in the moment, we run away to another world.

This book took you on a dark journey of unforgiving people, problems, and postulations.

And that's where any engaging story must start, avoiding the mundane and the ordinary, running from the realities of the now, and remembering better times where we were less concerned about a dad-gum twenty-four-hour news cycle, an unnecessary social media feed, or the world's unrest. For generations, people have been telling stories, and for generations, people have been enjoying them.

Let's simplify life a little and cut out the overload. Ladies, germs, and children, I hope you enjoyed this old-fashioned story of blood, guts, tears, and crazies. A mashup of summer fun mixed with autumn pleasures. So, whether you sipped a pumpkin spice latte, hung by the poolside, or slept with your lights on and the covers pulled over your head, may this story leave you with laughs, screams, and smiles.

Dan McDowell

ABOUT THE AUTHOR

Dan McDowell is a husband and father by day, and an author by night. The end result, chilling stories with gritty and real people facing unmistakable obstacles. With inspiration emerging from the best and the worst of Dan's nightmares, memories, and hyperactive imagination, he weaves tales of bizarre and intriguing proportions into a new stratosphere of descriptive writing that remains both distinct and thought provoking. He and his family currently reside in the San Antonio, TX, area.

NOTE FROM THE AUTHOR

Word-of-mouth is crucial for any author to succeed. If you enjoyed *Pool Man*, please leave a review online—anywhere you are able. Even if it's just a sentence or two. It would make all the difference and would be very much appreciated.

Thanks!
Dan McDowell

We hope you enjoyed reading this title from:

www.blackrosewriting.com

Subscribe to our mailing list – *The Rosevine* – and receive **FREE** books, daily deals, and stay current with news about upcoming releases and our hottest authors.
Scan the QR code below to sign up.

Already a subscriber? Please accept a sincere thank you for being a fan of Black Rose Writing authors.

View other Black Rose Writing titles at www.blackrosewriting.com/books and use promo code **PRINT** to receive a **20% discount** when purchasing.

www.ingramcontent.com/pod-product-compliance
Lightning Source LLC
Chambersburg PA
CBHW010736100726
47899CB00009B/3078